DENISE N. WHEATLEY

I Wish I Never Met You

DATING THE SHIFTLESS, STUPID, AND UGLY:

A NOVEL

A TOUCHSTONE BOOK
PUBLISHED BY SIMON & SCHUSTER
New York   London   Toronto   Sydney

A NOTE TO READERS
The author of this book has encountered many people through the years, and this story was inspired by some of the things that she has experienced. However, *I Wish I Never Met You* is a work of fiction, and none of those people is portrayed in this book. Names, characters, places, and incidents are either the product of the author's imagination or used fictitiously. Any resemblance to actual persons, living or dead, events, or locales is entirely coincidental.

TOUCHSTONE
Rockefeller Center
1230 Avenue of the Americas
New York, NY 10020

TOUCHSTONE and colophon are registered trademarks
of Simon & Schuster, Inc.

Designed by *Jan Pisciotta*

Manufactured in the United States of America

ISBN 0-7394-4506-5

To my mother,
for being the one thing in my life
that is perfect.

And to Stephanie Sherrer-Martin,
for your unconditional friendship
and endless support.

In certain trying circumstances, urgent circumstances, desperate circumstances, profanity furnishes a relief denied even to prayer.

—MARK TWAIN

CONTENTS

IV The Big Payback

I Wish
I Never
Met You

INTRO

It may be that your whole purpose in life
is simply to serve as a warning to others.
—Anonymous

I'm not saying I was always right. I'm not saying I was always wrong. What I am saying is that I always did what I felt in my heart at the time. People sometimes get caught up in the moment. Act without thinking. Do harmful things. Then live to regret them. Lucky for me, I'm not one of those people. When I take revenge, there are no regrets.

When it comes to certain situations, I have no conscience. I learn to accept and oftentimes welcome my vengeful behavior. Like the time when I set Dennis the Dumb-Ass Divorcé's apartment on fire. Or when I drop kicked and beat Cecil the Circus Midget in the middle of a crowded party. Or when I attacked Horace the Human Ape with my stun gun and blasted pepper spray inside his mouth. I could go on, but I don't want to reveal the entire contents of this book in the intro. My point is, I don't want you to pass judgment on my behavior until you know the whole story. Give me a chance. Find out how the dirty deeds of these people warranted my disinfecting behavior.

The thing is, I never wanted any trouble. All I wanted was to find a man. A husband. A soul mate. But for some reason, my search never led me to the promised land. Instead, I consistently fell into a deserted field of broken dreams and glass bottles.

Some may blame me. They may say that my chosen tactics were a little less than desirable. But I don't give a shit. It's over now. I've been had. I'm tired, sweaty, overworked, never paid, drained of all hope, and *still* single. That's depressing. I'm getting off the subject.

This book is not about singlehood. The book covers some of the ridiculous dating situations that I've gotten myself into and somehow got myself out of. If I hurt or humiliate anyone during the process of telling my story, too goddamn bad. My mission here is not to consider the feelings of those who have scorned me. My mission here is to offer a book that will act as a generous contribution from me to society. To provide a vital guide to what *not* to do when seeking a mate so that you won't make the same mistakes that I made. Walk down the same path of destruction that I laid. Go broke from the same huge prices that I paid. It wasn't worth it. It never is. So pay close attention.

For further guidance and understanding, I have concluded each chapter with an affirmation. A brief yet priceless affirmation that will encourage you to stop blaming yourself, the drugs, the alcohol, and the lack of sex (or too much bad sex) for your behavior. These critical affirmations will teach you who the hell to stay away from. You'll learn how good judgment alone can prevent you from performing senseless, damaging, life-threatening acts that you may one day live to regret. So if you do not comprehend the overall teachings within the chapters, you can always refer back to the affirmations at the end. Marvel at them. Memorize them. Live by them. Die by them. Ball them up and stuff them inside your brain. Share them with others. And you will never go wrong. Now on with the story . . .

I

One Night Only

The best love affairs are those we never had.

—NORMAN LINDSAY

One Night Only

There are those of us who love to go out and socialize. Toast with good alcohol. Dance to good music. Puff on good cigars. And, if appropriate, meet good potential mates. When the right encounter occurs, we unattached individuals are convinced that things will go from the exchanging of phone numbers to the first call to the first date to the first kiss to the first time to the first anniversary to the first wedding RSVP to the first baby carriage. Right?

Wrong. Doesn't always happen that way. Sometimes we may approach someone and not get any conversation whatsoever. If we do, we may not get the digits. If we do, we may not get the returned phone call. If we do, we may not get the first date. If we do, it may be a disaster. If it is, we never make it to the kiss, the sex, the wedding, or the baby carriage.

Then there are those of us who get tired of the random party scene. We are looking for an alternate route. So we abandon the barren bars and corny clubs. We decide to talk to family, friends, co-workers, and churchgoers to find out whether or not they know a good, compatible person to introduce us to. We listen closely to our options. We take our pick. We sit on the edge of our seats and wait for that initial phone call or e-mail. One of the two occurs. We love the conversation or message exchange. We anticipate that first date. We pray that this could be it. But what if it isn't?

If it isn't, we decide to hit the party scene again. But on a different level this time. We attend only events that are being thrown by someone we know. That way we already have an idea of what types will be in attendance. Hopefully we trust, admire, and respect the host or hostess. If we do, then we eagerly assume that the majority of his or her guests will be worthy of the same adulation. If we meet someone interesting, the ability to obtain a reliable reference is there. In case things don't work out with the person we've selected, we take mental notes of other options so we can ask about them later. But considering the faith that we've put into the host or hostess, we have already assumed that our first choice will probably work out. *Probably* is the operative word here.

If things don't work out, then we get tired of all forms of socialization. Period. All parties become superfluous. All matchmaking options have been exhausted. We decide to end our quest altogether. We stick to our regular routine and stop going out of our way to meet someone. But we still secretly hope that we'll experience a close encounter at the gas station, grocery store, health club, or church. That way, after telling everyone that we'd given up on relationships, we can lie and say that our furthest expectation was to find that special someone. We'd just been minding our business. Taking care of our affairs. Feeling content simply being alone. Then along came a miracle. Fate was on our side that day. Or was it?

As you will soon discover within the first three chapters of this book, nothing I just said really matters. It doesn't matter where or how you meet a person. Nothing is guaranteed. No territory is safe. The enemy could be lurking anywhere. Segregating sinners from do-gooders is illegal. So the boldest adulterers are still allowed to go to church. The most devious deceivers are still allowed to shop at the grocery store. The biggest liars are still allowed to work out at the gym. And the most despicable individuals are still allowed to befriend our matchmakers and pull off an unsuitable hookup.

I've run the gamut. I've been through it all. The parties, the matchmaking, the subconscious searches, and the letdowns. The situations where eager anticipation lasts so much longer than the actual event. How did I get through all of these ill-fated encounters and learn to prevent similar situations from occurring? Turn the page and find out.

Doug the Heinous Dragon

It was the worst blind date of my entire life. And believe me, I've been on some fucked-up blind dates. But this one took the cake. It all started the night I went to dinner with a married girlfriend of mine. As I sat there all night, complaining about the ridiculous men I'd been meeting, my girlfriend suggested that she introduce me to a wonderful man named Doug.

Doug was a great friend of hers who she'd worked with prior to meeting and marrying her husband. *Prior to meeting and marrying her husband*, I say. Question: If he was all that, why hadn't *she* gotten with him? As I wondered about this, my girl explained that since she and Doug had developed such a lovely working relationship/friendship, they'd decided to keep it that way. *Yeah, right.* I smelled a rat. But rather than exterminate the situation immediately, I foolishly opted to pinch my nose and allow the hookup to unfold.

According to my girlfriend, Doug was *the bomb*. He was in his mid-thirties, had a kind, generous personality, a great job, beautiful apartment, luxurious car, grand bank account, vast interests, impeccable wardrobe, active lifestyle, etc. Now, Doug wasn't "a looker," as my friend put it. But he was tall, husky like a football player, attractive enough, and very well put together. "Perfect" to be exact. I told my friend that he did indeed sound like a great guy. Plus, tall, husky, football player look-alikes need love too, right? And since my girlfriend was very attractive, intelligent, kind, and God-fearing, I trusted that she could rate our compatibility well and use good judgment. My now overly excited girlfriend said that she'd call Doug that night and arrange for him to contact me.

Doug e-mailed me the following Monday. His message was articulate, and he sounded interesting and distinguished. After exchanging several messages, I was looking forward to meeting him later on that week. But he was facing a very busy schedule and put me off until later on that following week. I figured that big Doug must have it going in a big way, putting *me* off like that. But the dis extended my anticipation even further.

During the middle of that next week, Doug and I made plans to meet after work at a Mexican restaurant that was close to both of our jobs. Since I took the train in, darling Doug offered to take me home after dinner. I declined at first, thinking that might be a bit much. But he insisted that it would be no trouble at all. When I remembered how my girlfriend had described him, I finally agreed. After all, if things went as I hoped they would, maybe we'd go somewhere after dinner and I'd invite him up for a drink afterward.

At last, the day of our date arrived. I took a change of clothes to work so that I'd be so fresh and so clean for this one. I had to come correct. The workday dragged on for what seemed like sixteen hours, as opposed to the normal eight. By the time five o' clock finally rolled around, I was anxious and nervous as hell. I charged to the bathroom to begin my trans-formation. I emerged laced in a dazzling sleeveless silk ice-blue Armani blouse and flowing cream pants. My strappy sandals were severely heeled. My hair was simply flipped, and my makeup was freshly applied. I hate to brag, but my shit was tight.

I felt like a movie star when I stepped from my building and into a cab. It was hot as hell, but I was confident that the extra blot powder, deodorant, and perfume that I'd applied would preserve my look and aroma. People were staring. My hair and pants were swaying in the wind. My nerves were buzzing around the pit of my stomach like bees in a hive. I was scared. What if Doug didn't like me? What if he didn't think I was good enough for him? What if my conversation didn't appeal to him?

Many more thoughts of insecurity had flown through my mind by the time the cab pulled up in front of the restaurant. I paid the driver and stepped out into the dense heat. I thought about just going home. Social outings weren't supposed to make me feel this sick and distressed. But it was too late to turn back now. Doug was probably waiting for me. My girlfriend was probably depending on me. Plus, as panicky as I was, I really didn't want to leave. This could be it. This one could right all of the previous wrongs. But there was only one way to find out. So I inhaled deeply, hoping that the hot summer oxygen would calm my jagged nerves, and walked into the restaurant.

I looked around for Doug. I saw no one that should have been Doug. The only thing I saw was some hugely oversized man staring intently at a menu hanging from the wall. He looked over and smiled at me. I just stood there and stared at him. Eventually, after he wouldn't take his eyes off me, I acknowledged him with a nod of my head and looked around again for Doug.

Other than the hugely oversized man, the place was empty. But the hugely oversized man couldn't be Doug. Because Doug was husky like a football player, not fat like a pregnant woman headed straight for the delivery room after passing her due date by ten months. Doug was well groomed, not shabby and ashy with a neckline that ended somewhere in the middle of his back. Doug dressed impeccably. So I knew that he wouldn't be caught dead in a tight ass, dusty, used-to-be-white-but-now-it's-gray, Catholic school uniform shirt, moth-eaten pants that used to be black but now are also gray because they've been washed too many goddamn times, thick ass, faded black sweat socks, and flat, beat-up, run-over, soleless, navy blue shoes similar to the ones worn by Dorothy's mother on *The Golden Girls*.

The Doug I'd heard about wouldn't have been caught dead rocking bifocals as thick as his ass that tightly clutched a face reminiscent of Professor Klump's in *The Nutty Professor*. And he wouldn't dare wear a paper-thin nylon coat that wasn't long, wasn't short, wasn't any sort of length you've ever seen. It was a coat that just fell somewhere in the middle of his ham-hocked, knock-kneed, overstuffed thighs.

I convulsed and almost cried as this hugely oversized man came bobbling over toward me. *Run*, I thought to myself immediately. *He doesn't know who you are yet, so just run!* But I didn't want to do my girlfriend like that (even though the bitch had done me like this).

The hugely oversized man approached me and introduced himself. He was indeed Doug. His high-pitched voice squeaked around his lispy tongue. When I managed to ask how he was doing, he giggled, wheezed, and just shook his hugely sloped head. The rolls on the back of his neck did the jitterbug. At that very moment, I suffered a mental breakdown, but I somehow kept my composure. *I've been bamboozled*, I thought to myself as I watched the mountain of flesh hanging from Doug's chin and neck jiggle with excitement. I just gave him a strained smile, turned toward the hostess, and reluctantly asked for a table for two.

I walked through the restaurant and prayed that I wouldn't see anyone I knew. If I did, I would swear Doug was my uncle. I stared at my feet and wondered where I'd gone wrong. As my eyes locked with the fiery red Spanish tiles that lined the restaurant floor, I connected with the flames in hell. *What had I done to deserve this, Lord?* I asked myself. I was a good person, prayed every night, treated others as I wanted to be treated, all that. So why was this happening to me? Why was I suffering this diabolical damnation?

When Doug and I sat down, I got the close up view. And it was worse than I'd thought. His teeth were unlike anything I'd ever seen before. Well, maybe they resembled something I'd witnessed on *Wild Discovery*. Doug's teeth were very, very small and very, very sharp. And there were so *many* of them. So many that they had formed their own rows of existence. They were the teeth of a piranha. The type of teeth that would fuck you up to the bone if you dare upset or attack their owner.

And Doug was sick. Not sick in the head, but sick with a cold. It was 110 degrees in the shade and this man had somehow managed to get ill. He called it a "slight cold." Along with his "slight cold" came a mucus-filled chest, extensive wheezing, and major coughing. Along with all of that physical exertion in the sweltering heat came sweat. And not just regular sweat. I'm talking about that sick-ass, VapoRub, heating-pad, soggy-bathrobe type of sweat. And along with all that sick-ass sweat came a pungent odor that oozed through Doug's damp, infected pores. Bottom line, I was in a fucked up situation that I didn't know how to get out of. If I left, I'd be rude and mean. If I stayed, I'd slit my wrist with my butter knife. I was stuck. In the end, I decided to just stay. What doesn't kill you only makes you stronger, right? When you get lemons, make lemonade, right? I know. That bullshit never worked for me either.

Throughout dinner, Doug's clammy, stale, musty aroma burned the hairs that lined the insides of my nostrils. (I know because the ashes fell into my plate.) In between his phlegm-filled whooping coughs, I had to hear about his cheap-ass apartment out in the suburbs, his data-entry club, the little girl from church who he didn't want to give singing lessons to on weekends but did anyway because he'd promised her mother he would, his brother's kids, his cousin's reptiles, his bowling league, etc. I didn't give a damn about anything he was talking about. Doug was a very uninteresting man. I found myself talking about sports and anything else that would keep me awake throughout this smelly, hellish experience.

Finally, dinner was over. But was it really?

"So, do you wanna take a walk?" Doug snorted.

I gasped in horror. *A walk?* Was he crazy? I sat there with my mouth hanging open, my eyes darting from side to side, not knowing how to appropriately address such an absurd question.

"My car is parked about three blocks away from here. Wanna walk?" he wheezed.

I breathed a sigh of relief after realizing that he didn't mean a romantic walk, then decided to walk to the car with Doug in order to help speed up this funky situation.

When we got outside, I began walking at what I thought was a normal pace. But as Doug rambled on about his data-entry club, I noticed that he was several steps behind me, hobbling along and breathing quite heavily. I caught the hint and slowed down so that Big Daddy could catch up. When he did, I turned my head in the opposite direction so that I wouldn't have to inhale the putrefied odor coming from his bacteria-infested system. Yet as Doug's paper-thin coat blew fiercely in the hot wind, the pungency emitted at an even more alarming rate. I swallowed continuously in order to stop the bile that kept creeping up in my throat.

As we continued walking for what seemed like forever, Doug began talking about the data-entry club's membership roster. I sang old Negro spirituals to myself in hopes that some of my ancestors' strength would rub off on me. When we finally arrived at the car, my eyes began to tear up at the mere thought of having to sit so close to Doug and his stench.

Once inside, I quickly rolled my window down and stuck my head out of it, acting as if I was truly enjoying a view that I'd seen a thousand times before. Doug told me he could turn the air on, but I insisted that I preferred fresh air. There was no way in hell I was going to sit in that car with the windows rolled up and allow Doug's funk to continuously circulate and violently suffocate me.

As Doug rattled on about absolutely nothing, I absentmindedly threw in an "Aha" here or an "Uh-huh" there, whenever it seemed appropriate. I was just glad that the date was almost over. I thought about what I would tell my girlfriend the next day. "Thanks, but no thanks," or "Rot in hell, bitch." Considering how much she cared about Doug, I decided to try to be nice about the whole thing.

Now, here's the kicker. When we arrived at my building, I knew this man was not going to try to kiss me, come upstairs, or anything like that. But what he did do was even more asinine as far as I was concerned. Doug pulled up to the curb, put the car in park, turned to me, and smiled that spiked-tooth smile. Then he wheezed, "Now, when you talk to our friend tomorrow, tell her that I worked out for the past two days straight, shaved, and wore my Sunday best!"

"Oh, uh, okay," I stammered, struggling to find the damn door handle.

"I'll be in touch," Doug assured me, shaking his head and jiggling the pork hanging from his chin and neck.

"Okay," I repeated, already out of the car. I broke ass toward my building before he could say anything else. I walked through my lobby and felt like vomiting. I'd been shocked into a hypothermic state. I was numb. Gangrene was setting in. I felt cold and desperate and vulnerable, like my world was coming to an end. I had no backup plan. No B, C, *or* D plan man to turn to. I had to figure out a way to shake this hopeless feeling off me.

As I walked through my apartment door, everything looked different. My world was now tainted. I felt dejected, yet relieved. I was finally away from that man. He was behind me now. I had no one to turn to, but at least I could start over again. I immediately picked up the phone and called one of my best friends, who'd been waiting anxiously to hear about the date. As I filled her in on the gruesome details, she laughed so hard she cried. "On to the next," I said as we attempted to run through a list of other bleak-to-nonexistent options.

The next day, the girlfriend who'd hooked Doug and me up e-mailed me first thing in the morning and asked how my "meeting" had gone. Oh, so suddenly we had gone from a date to a meeting, huh? The fool must have realized the huge mistake she'd made.

The "meeting" was okay, but Doug and I didn't seem to have much in common, I replied.

That was good, wasn't it? Not mean, but firm enough to let the girl know where Doug and I stood. Nowhere. She caught the hint quickly and never mentioned his name again.

Bottom Damn Line: Fuck a blind date.

Preston the Project Mishap

ave you ever been through a drought? Not just a regular, few-weeks-to-a-few-months type of drought. I'm talking about a full-blown, detrimental, all-out *drought*. One of those droughts where you ain't had none and you *know* you ain't finna get none. One of those droughts that has you shuffling through your tore-up-ass phone book over and over again, only to find that you *still* have no one to call. A drought that has you contemplating calling an escort service. A drought that has you pissing dust. Have you ever been through one of those? I have. And it ain't nothing to fuck with.

I'll never forget it. It was one of the toughest times of my life. I couldn't figure out where I had gone wrong. One minute I was the number one draft pick. The summa of the cum laudes. The Oscar of the award shows. I was the end-all. I was the be-all. Basically what I'm trying to say is, I was the shit. Then one day, out of nowhere, *Bam!* I lost it.

That glimmer in my eye suddenly vanished. That *certain something* I had once possessed did an about-face. I had played myself out. No one was calling. Invitations had stopped coming. Everyone had moved on and left me behind. Nobody missed me. I had become a has-been. It didn't feel good.

So I crawled into a hole and didn't beg to come back. I had everyone thinking I'd elevated to another level. I didn't look over my shoulder, for that would only slow me down. I forged ahead quickly and found new friends. I enjoyed their company. I forgot about the good ole days and looked to create new ones. But something was missing. It took me a split second to figure it out. It was a man.

I was no longer pulling 'em in like I used to. I no longer possessed the Midas touch. Now everything I touched turned to shit instead of gold. I had no mack. My game was wack. Men ran from me, laughed at me, dissed me, and ignored me. I was a virus. I had been cursed. I had been condemned to spending the rest of my life alone.

So I stopped dead in my tracks. I had to. I needed to figure out where I'd gone wrong. I finally turned around and looked over my shoulder. I blocked my eyes from all the sunny memories that stood in the road. A teardrop descended. I stood there and studied my past. I suddenly realized what had changed. It wasn't the people around me. It was me. I had become ready for bigger. I had become ready for better. I had wanted something more. I had wanted something deeper. Deeper than drinking. Deeper than smoking. Deeper than screwing. Deeper than idle gossip. I had subconsciously surpassed my former life. The good-time girl had left the building. The teardrops ceased. I accepted my situation, turned back around, and kept on moving.

My mental map read that I was in the middle of a transformation, a metamorphosis, a soaring journey. My plane was still in midflight. The motion sickness was rough as hell. But I got over it. I knew that my current loneliness wasn't a tragedy. It was a blessing in disguise. All of the negligent men had actually done me a favor. They'd allowed me to journey deep into the forest, alone, and rediscover myself. Redevelop myself. Reinvent myself. Reevaluate myself. When I reentered the world, I was a stronger, wiser, cooler, calmer, more together individual.

One day my girlfriend called to congratulate me on my rebirth. Then she invited me to a birthday party that a friend of hers was throwing. The party was at a hot new spot. The crowd would not remind me of the olden days. The guy throwing the party was a good catch who she'd been friends with for years. He was attractive, popular, highly educated, and possessed a great personality. He was well off and partic-ipated in various community-service projects. All of his friends would be there. They would all be just like him. This party sounded as if it could be the perfect thirst quencher for a renewed yet parched woman such as myself.

I dressed conservatively in a fitted gray sweater and slacks. I wanted men to meet my inner being before getting all acquainted with my physical attributes. My friend picked me up and told me I looked like an attractive, intelligent, successful individual. *Good*, I thought. That's exactly what I was looking to attract.

When we walked into the club, a cloud of putrid, Frito-laced, bodussy-type smog hit me dead in the face. My makeup rotted immediately. My curls fizzled simultaneously. I had transformed into Sho'nuff from *The Last Dragon* before we even reached the bar. But I was unfazed, because my spiritual being was shining through and through.

Then I remembered that God wants us to be at our best at all times. So I fled to the bathroom and attempted to fix myself up as much as possible. I grabbed a wad of toilet paper and blotted the bottom of my raccoon eyes and the borders of my smudged lips. I dampened a paper towel and absorbed curdled concealer. I pulled my hair behind my ears, fluffed up the back, and fronted like I had a fresh roller set. Then I applied some powder, reglossed my lips, and headed back upstairs to find me somebody.

My girlfriend and I sat down at the bar and ordered drinks. I got cranberry juice because I was feeling extra deep that night and didn't want to intoxicate the vibe. Then I saw a man eyeing me who resembled a buffalo butt. My vibe got inebriated immediately. I ducked down on my stool and spun around in hopes that he would catch the hint and forget about me.

When I did, my eyes fell upon the most delicious, delectable-looking delicatessen imaginable. This man was so fine that I wanted to lay him down on a kaiser roll and bite the shit out of him. He was standing at the bar a few stools away, ordering a drink and laughing his pretty ass off. I wanted to get in on the joke. His smooth, perfect, brown-cocoa skin and clean, bald head glowed underneath the disco lights. He had one hand in the pocket of his navy blue slacks and the other waving in the air, trying to flag down the bartender. I could see muscles bulging through his blazer. He carried himself like a down-to-earth celebrity. I wanted to go over and ask for an autograph. He got his drink. He smiled real big and laughed real hard before walking away. I lost him in the crowd. I started to pout.

My girlfriend got up to dance with the birthday boy. I was jealous. I wanted to dance with somebody, too. Then the buffalo butt who'd been eyeing me earlier came over and started talking to me. He looked like a broke-ass Bookman from *Good Times*. He smelled like a broke ass Bookman after repairing the Evanses' broke-ass toilet. His teeth were thick and crusty. His ass was fat and lopsided. His girlie Afro looked like it had been set with pink sponge rollers and pink setting lotion. He looked nothing like my superstar. I was anxious for him to get the hell away from me. He asked if I wanted to dance. I told him I was gay and that my big, strong girlfriend would be back any minute. He told me that I needed Jesus and stomped off. I felt the floor shake.

Then my superstar walked back up. He was standing only two stools away now, grabbing some napkins. I started to tingle inside. He looked over at me. I kept staring at him. My heart skipped to the beat of the bass line in the background. My vibe sobered back up. Then my girlfriend came over after her long, dirty dance with the birthday boy and interrupted my visual conversation. She was happy as hell and anxious to share all the details. There were no more stools available, so I scooted over and let her share mine. She put her arm around me so as not to fall off. I put my arm around her so as not to fall off. Her mouth was close to my ear as she told her tale over the loud music. I giggled with excitement after she mentioned wanting to take the birthday boy home at the end of the night. We both did a little victory wiggle in our seat. Bookman walked by. He glared at us, then felt compelled to stop and come over.

"That's a damn shame," he sputtered, shaking his head shamefully. "Two beautiful women, just gone to waste! The

Lord rebukes this type of behavior, you know." Then he shot us a look of disgrace and walked away.

"What the hell was that all about?" my girlfriend yelled.

"I'll tell you later," I yelled back as I spotted my superstar sitting on a nearby couch. Alone. "I'll be right back."

As I walked over to the couch, I reminded myself that I was a new woman. I was stronger, bolder, calmer, and all that good stuff. I was also wise enough to know good stock when I saw it. And this specimen I'd been studying all night was the real thing. He was no jive turkey. He was 100 percent pure grade A beef. I let no inhibitions cross my mind as I stepped to him like a renewed woman should.

"Hello." I smiled, sitting down next to him.

"Hi." He smiled back, looking like a man who belonged on the cover of a magazine. I offered my hand and introduced myself.

"I'm Preston," he said as he shook my hand firmly. "How are you?"

"I'm fine," I answered, noticing that his grin was shy and his eye contact was bashful. It was the sweetest thing I'd ever known. I was humbling this big, strong, gorgeous man. The thought of an eradicated drought crossed my mind. I wet my dried-up mouth with my juice in anticipation.

Preston and I indulged in an intriguing conversation. First we talked religion. He seemed extremely enlightened and close with God. He taught the Bible to his friends and urged them to attend church. He didn't eat pork, which I thought was deep as hell, with my ham sandwich-eating ass. I told him I'd tried to stop a couple of times and just couldn't do it. He recommended several Scriptures to read for strength and guidance. I wrote them down. Then he recommended that I write his phone number down too. I turned into a feline in heat as the thought of clawing his clothes off crossed my mind.

After I jotted down his number, we began to talk politics and dissected the bizarre 2000 presidential election. We talked occupation and activity. Preston had a job at a not-for-profit organization that worked with inner-city schools and youth centers. In his free time, he worked toward becoming a professional bodybuilder. In my free time, I worked toward becoming a professional stalker. I'd just found my new client. I didn't tell him that, though. Next we talked relationships. I mentioned being single and childless. He mentioned being childless. Then he mentioned his girl-friend of thirteen months.

I bid adieu and got up to walk away. He grabbed my arm and asked me to sit back down. He told me that he loved my conversation and wanted to get to know me better. He told me we had connected on a mental and spiritual level. He told me he didn't want me to worry about his situation. I told him I was tired of driving down dead-end streets. He told me he stayed on a main thoroughfare. I told him that was corny as hell. He laughed and asked for my phone number. I laughed and told him I'd have to think about it. He stared at me quietly through his dark, intense, almond-shaped eyes. I stared back. My insides quivered. I accidentally laid my hand on his thigh. I felt a strong, hard, bulging muscle. "It's 555-1348," I rattled off quickly.

Preston's friends came over and told him they were ready to go. He said okay and told them that he'd be out in a minute. Then he turned to me, kissed my cheek lightly, and promised to call. As soon as he was out the door, my girl, some associates, and some women I didn't even know came swarming over. Everybody had been talking about how fine Preston was all night. They were all jealous of my good fortune. They insisted that I'd just met my husband, my soldier, my *soul* mate. I verbally told them to calm down and mentally agreed with them all. I accidentally forgot to tell them that he had a girlfriend. But I did remember to thank them for their good wishes. I knew this was it. I could *feel* it. My long, drought-filled hiatus was finally over.

Preston called me early the next afternoon. I was one frantic human being. No words could describe the feelings fluttering throughout my body. It was surreal. I had suddenly gained a sixth sense. I could smell happiness and hear passion and touch contentment and taste intimacy. I didn't care about his girlfriend anymore. I didn't care about anything anymore. I wanted to run off and elope at that exact moment.

Preston asked me to come over for lunch. *He gets right to the point*, I thought as I quickly jotted down his address. I was a little familiar with the general area and told him I could probably be there in about an hour. He blew me a kiss through the phone. I opened my mouth wide and sucked it right out of the receiver.

I hung up the phone and thought about my mission. I couldn't half-step on this one. I had to knock this girlfriend of thirteen months out the box. So I pulled out my treasure chest of best and rifled through its contents. My sheer black Ralph Lauren dress with the soft, flowing ruffle at the plunging V-neckline and asymmetrical hem seemed suitable for the occasion. I unwrapped my snakeskin stilettos. I took a quick hot shower and massaged shimmering iridescent lotion into my skin. I sprayed my pulse points with a heavily alluring perfume. I recurled my hair even though it wasn't necessary, dusted bronzing powder over my face, coated my lashes with dark brown mascara, and dabbed peachy gloss on my lips. I dressed quickly and accidentally forgot to put on undergarments. I did a quick once-over in the mirror. I looked ravishing and inviting and dehydrated. I left my building, wondering if I'd just take a sip or drink the whole damn bottle.

I was nervous in a good, anxious kind of way during the drive to Preston's house. The thrill of the whole thing tickled at my skin. I couldn't wait to see him again and enjoy our privacy, revel in our chemistry, and taste his kisses. My skin felt the urge to lie in his bed and roll around in his sheets. This was unlike anything I'd ever known. It was where I wanted to be.

I was so deep in lust that I missed Preston's street. I looked around and saw nothing but desolation. A few leafless trees here, a few grassless plots of land there. Suddenly, I approached a dead end. I was so far over on one side of the city that I couldn't go any farther. I hadn't seen his street. I made a U-turn and backtracked slowly. Still, nothing but desolation. When I pulled out my cell phone and tried to call

Preston, my battery died as I dialed. I decided to keep driving around until I found his street. I was trying to get my engagement on. Finally, after another twenty minutes, I approached his block.

The memory of that screeching left turn I made onto West Hell Avenue still brings me to chilling tears. I drove slowly down the block and watched in amazement as dirty, destitute, poverty-stricken people roamed the streets. Degenerates, both young and old, covered every single piece of cement on that block. Potholes so deep, so obese began to attack my tires. The ferocious impact jolted my body up and down and back and forth like a fucking bucking bronco. Whiplash began to ensue.

I glared out the window and was greeted by several horrifyingly gruesome sights. Endless rows of raggedy, run-down, doorless, graffiti-infested, housing projects lined the block. Gangbangers in fake-ass MCM jogging suits rocked fat gold chains and fat gold teeth. They sat on the hoods of their hydraulic and chrome-laced vehicles, cleaning guns and blasting music loud enough to be heard anywhere within the United States. Indiscreet drug dealers in bathrobes and house shoes were selling plastic vials of crack to decrepit, disoriented, grimy-bra- and ragged-panty-wearing hypes. Some begged to have the hit put on their tabs. Others opted to crawl around haphazardly on their raw hands and scabby knees, combing the asphalt for fallen drug residue.

Toothless, crusty-lipped, two-bit hustlers in shorts and dress shoes were selling *Asses of XXXtasy* porno tapes, Polish sausages, and body oils. Dirty, shabby, half-dressed children who hadn't been introduced to lotion were playing a game called "Hit Me, Bitch," where they ran in front of moving cars and dared the drivers to run them over. Filthy, three-legged, one-eyed animals with patches of missing skin limped up and down the street with a democracy all their own.

Pimps in wrinkled-up mom-and-pop suits with processed hair, long manicured nails, fake alligator shoes, and tons of phony jewels leaned against their flashy cars and lectured the pimps-in-training. Overweight, bucktoothed, orange wig-wearing, hairy, pockmarked prostitutes were complaining that their backs and feet were killing them. The pimps politely excused themselves from their lesson, gave the street-walkers a quick beat down, told them to go back out and get the rest of their money, then went right back to their lectures.

Sheer disbelief is what I felt. I panicked. I hyperventi-lated. I choked on my own saliva. My lungs were constrict-ing and filling up with thick cotton. I needed an inhaler and I don't have asthma. I didn't know what to do. I prayed that these people didn't see me. I didn't quite fit in there. The address Preston had given me was hanging upside down on one of the row houses. I imagined how these people would react if I parked my car and got out. The concept froze me over. I couldn't call the police to come and save me because my phone battery was dead. I was in what you could easily call a fucked up situation.

I wanted to turn around and go home, but I didn't want to hurt Preston's feelings. Then the more I thought about it, the more I began to dislike Preston. Why hadn't he warned me about what I was getting ready to roll into? Why didn't he tell me he lived at the Crenshaw Swap Meet? Why didn't he advise me to come through in my fur Kangol, '85 Gremlin, and Fila snaps? Since he hadn't, I decided not to give a damn about his feelings. Besides, if I stayed, I might as well have just stripped down my own car and given up my own ass. If the crackheads didn't rob me, the children would beat me. If the gangbangers didn't shoot me, the pimps would put me to work. It was a lose-lose situation.

As I cursed the fact that I'd agreed to visit Preston, the Children of the Corn began to surround my car. They looked as if they were going to beat and eat me. So I did what any sensible human being would do in a situation like this. I put the pedal to the metal and hauled ass out of there. But when I got to the end of the block, a No Outlet sign stood bold as shit. I wanted to cry. Preston had lied to me. He *did* stay on a dead-end street.

I contemplated having to turn around and drive back down West Hell Avenue. The anticipation caused a series of seizures. I stuck a spoon in my mouth and turned around anyway. My eyes were met with a ghastly sight. The Children of the Corn, along with the insane animal posse, had gathered in the middle of the street. The evil kids were smiling demonically and waiting for me to come back so they could kill me. Bats and sticks and knives were waving in the air. Cockeyed animals were yelping and hopping around on their one good leg. I began to recite the Hail Mary.

Then I made a decision. It took only a split second. I rammed the accelerator through the floor of my car and hit every last motherfucker standing in that street. The severe impact caused the juvenile delinquents to cling to my windshield wipers, grip my sunroof, and grasp my side-view mirrors. Diseased animals clawed at my windows and snarled with rotten, cracked teeth at me through the glass. I slammed down on the brakes just long enough to unleash the dragons, then slammed down on the gas again.

I finally reached the other end of the block. God was giving me a second chance at life. But everything would be different now. I would have to live life as a murderer, a sinner, a witch who should be hung by a jury of my peers. I needed to go repent. I breathed in through my nose and out through my mouth several times in order to try to calm my nerves. Then I reluctantly glanced in my rearview mirror, petrified of all the damage that I'd done.

My eyes were met with yet another amazing sight. Every last child and animal that I'd struck was getting up off the ground. They began dusting themselves off and walking back towards the curb. Then they started repositioning themselves and their weapons, eagerly anticipating their next contestant. The rest of the block remained unfazed as well. The pimps were still pimping, the hustlers were still hustling, the prostitutes were still complaining, the hypes were still smoking, and the gangbangers were now shooting. The whole scene was too ridiculous to believe. So I decided not to. I would bury the whole experience and act as if it had never, ever happened. I would mention it to no one. And I would never speak to Preston again.

On the way home I stopped by the hardware store. I bought a heavy-duty toilet plunger and an industrial-size bottle of Liquid-Plumr in order to prepare for the dust that would continue to fall from my body and clog up my toilet for the time being. I, the renewed woman, was a bit disoriented by the whole ordeal but still intact. And so was my dreadful, *painful* drought.

> **Bottom Damn Line:** Fuck a man who will cheat on his girlfriend. He'll also jeopardize your safety.

Ernest the Undercover Sugarbooty

Have you ever met a man who wore a thong underneath his boxers? I have. His name was Ernest, and he was a surefire undercover sugarbooty. Debonair and in search of a fly girl on the outside, yet feeble and longing for a strong man's touch on the inside. Limp dick, wobbly wrists, fluid hips, and flimsy lips. The best gossiper you know (he'll keep you on the phone for hours), the best dresser you know, wears the best cologne, keeps his nails tight, fade like *whoa*, soft and gentle hands, gets invited to all the elite parties, and can dance his ass off? Don't believe the hype. You dun caught chu a sugarbooty.

I met Ernest in a record store during one of my tired-of-looking-for-a-man phases. The last thing on my mind was meeting someone (supposedly). I just wanted to pick up a few CDs. I was heading toward the hip-hop section of the store when I first caught sight of Ernest. He was scanning the disco music section. He looked up and we made eye contact. He smiled, I smiled, and his eyes followed me as I sauntered past him. Ernest was cute as hell, with smooth tawny skin, luscious lips, and dark, penetrating eyes. He was dressed in a creamy cashmere turtleneck, chocolate brown leather pants, and a matching leather jacket. His curly locks were neatly faded, and his silver jewelry was shining just as bright as his dreamy smile.

I reached the back of the store and began scanning the CDs, fronting like I was really preoccupied and wasn't thinking about this slim who was eyeing my back. Then the next thing I knew, he came up behind me and spoke.

"Hey," he said, his voice smooth and deep. *Damn*, he had me fooled.

"Hello," I purred, turning around slowly and smiling seductively. I prayed that he didn't think I sounded as stupid as I knew I did. Eroticism has never been one of my specialties.

"I hope you don't mind my saying this, but you're very sexy," he said, his intense stare singeing my soul. *Good*. I had his ass fooled, too.

"Well, thank you," I replied.

"I'm Ernest," he said, holding out his soft, subtle hand. "I'm so pleased to meet you."

"Likewise," I responded, so mesmerized that I didn't realize that I was gripping his hand much, much harder than he was gripping mine.

"What have you got there?" he asked, looking down at the CDs in my hand.

"Oh, I'm just adding to my hip-hop collection," I said, nervously fidgeting through the CDs in my hand. "I've got Lil' Kim, Wu-Tang Clan, and an old school Too Short album. What are you getting?"

"Well, I'm not big on rap music. I've got Donna Summer's *Bad Girls*, Gloria Gaynor's *I Will Survive*, and Diana Ross's *I'm Coming Out*," he boasted.

For some reason this didn't strike me as odd. Maybe it was because I was too busy trying to mack.

"Ohh, I like those songs," I cooed, grabbing Ernest's arm in excitement.

"Well, if you like disco music, we should exchange numbers. I've got an extensive collection at home. Do you like to go out?"

"Yeah, I'm out almost every weekend. I'll give you my number."

"Cool," Ernest said as he pulled out his Palm Pilot. I gave him my number, and he told me he would call soon, then walked away.

I could no longer feel my feet touch the floor after our encounter. I ran home, told all my friends about Ernest, then looked through my closet trying to figure out what I'd wear when we hooked up. I knew I'd have to have my shit together with a man like Ernest because he was the type who'd be out here looking better than me, and I wasn't having that. So I selected my flashy, high-class call-girl getup, which consisted of a short, sleeveless silver metal dress and sparkling, high, high heels.

Ernest called the next day and invited me to a private listening party that weekend. I felt so privileged. I was so excited. If only I'd known then what I know now. He picked me up on Saturday night and showed me the time of my life. We laughed, drank, danced, drank, dogged out everyone's outfits, drank, cuddled occasionally, and drank all night. The thing I loved most was how Ernest made me dance so much more spectacularly than normal. He had me pulling moves out of my ass that I'd never known were there. I guess I mistook his talent for chemistry. Nevertheless, folks were calling me Janet as I drunkenly hobbled out the door.

When we got to the car, Ernest opened my door and said, "I'm loving you in that dress."

"Thank you," I slurred, stepping in and flashing entirely too much thigh.

"Is that Dior?" he asked, getting in and starting the engine.

"Galliano." I smiled, flattered that he'd asked. *Flattered.* Not curious as to why he gave a shit. Just *flattered.*

"*Sooo,* what do you wanna do now?" Ernest asked.

It was 3:45 in the morning. Our choices were extremely limited. "I don't know, Ernest. It's so *late.* What do you suggest?" I asked with a wide-eyed look of dumb innocence. I was so phony. I knew good and damn well I wanted to go back to his house and get busy.

"We're having such a good time, why don't you come over so I can show you my record collection?" Ernest suggested.

Jackpot! "You won't mind taking me home after that?" I asked, as if I really were concerned.

"No, I won't mind. But you're more than welcome to stay if you want," Ernest replied, his eyes on the road the whole time. "It'll be like a sleepover."

"Hmmm," I stalled, like I really needed to think about it. "Okay, that'll work," I finally said. Then, as I looked out the window, making sure Ernest could see nothing but the back of my head, I closed my eyes real tight and grinned harder than ever. I was frantic as hell. Ernest had stirred up an enormous amount of sexual tension within me during all that drinking and bumping and grinding. Now that the foreplay was out of the way, there was nothing left to do but one thing and one thing only.

When we got to Ernest's house, he led me straight into his exquisitely decorated bedroom. I stared at the dramatic abstract artwork hanging from his milky-white silk walls. I felt as if I were walking on a white sandy beach as my heels sank down low into his plush pale carpeting. I wasted no time. I immediately fell onto his big, fluffy bed. His soft suede comforter felt like a texturized cloud floating underneath me. The ton of pale pillows propped up against Ernest's huge, white, vinelike headboard matched his bed skirt and drapes. I kicked off my shoes, wiggled my pedicured toes in anticipation, and watched as Ernest sifted through a crate of records that I was totally uninterested in.

"I've got it all, girl," he said feverishly. "You got any requests?"

Yeah, for you to get your ass in this bed and fuck me, the liquor and I wanted to say. But instead we said, "How about my theme song, 'Bad Girls'?" I hoped he'd catch the hint. He didn't.

"Okay!" he responded enthusiastically, throwing the record on and turning the volume up all the way.

Okay, maybe he'll come over here when the record starts playing, I thought. He didn't. Ernest totally ignored me as I licked my lips and caressed my hips. He danced right past me and plopped down onto an ivory chaise lounge in the corner of the room. Then he closed his eyes and started bobbing his head to the music.

I couldn't believe it. Why wasn't he lying here next to me? What the hell was this world coming to? I was confused and upset and about to get irate. But you know what they say to do when you start feeling this way. They say don't do anything. Just wait until you're calm and have come to your senses. So I waited. And I waited. And I waited. Finally, after about forty-five damn minutes and forty-five more songs, I just couldn't wait any longer. I got up, went over to the chaise, and sat down next to Ernest. His eyes were still closed, and the music was so loud that he hadn't heard me coming.

As I sat there staring enticingly at him, my mouth started watering. I wanted to grab that sweet neck and suck it for dear life. I wanted to throw my legs over his hips and shove my tongue down his throat. These violent sexual urges were scaring and exciting me all at the same time. The only thing left to do was make my move. But of course, *of course*, after that long ass record had played all goddamn night, it decided to stop right at that very moment. When Ernest opened his eyes and saw me sitting there with lust all in my face, he gasped and jumped away.

"You *scared* me!" he proclaimed, gripping his chest with a look of pure horror on his face.

"Why, did you forget I was here or something?" I asked, totally taken aback by his reaction.

"No, it's just that you were all the way on the other side of the room, that's all." Ernest pointed as he got up and turned off the record player.

Am I missing something? I asked myself, totally baffled. I just sat there, secretly trying to sniff underneath my arms and figure out where I'd gone wrong. Then, after confirming that I smelled just fine, that irate feeling started setting in again.

"You ready to go?" Ernest asked, handing me my purse.

Go? I had just gotten there! I'd thought we were going to have a sleepover! I had to do something. I had to erase these feelings of desperation and dejection. I had to turn this situation around. It was now or never. I had to be aggressive. My future started here. I had to be all that I could be. All those bullshit military-type mottoes started flying through my head. So my dumb ass decided to get up and follow them.

"No, actually I'm not ready to go," I whispered, sensually walking toward him. I snatched my Louis Vuitton out of his hand and flung it down on the floor. I grabbed him by the shoulders and flung him down onto the bed. I abruptly climbed on top of him, unbuckled his belt, and unfastened his pants. I kissed him more passionately than I'd ever kissed a man before. I grabbed the sides of that precious face, fondled his tender tongue with mine, and sucked on those pouty lips. I threw his shirt up over his head and tickled his pink nipples with my fingertips. I stuck my hand down his pants and clasped his soft, limp, flubbery little morsel. I was absolutely out of control. I was a dominatrix, longing for my skintight black patent-leather catsuit, wooden paddle, and cat-o'-nine-tails.

Suddenly Ernest grabbed me by my waist and threw me onto the other side of the bed. "What are you *doing*?" he insisted, frantically fastening his pants and shoving his arms back into his shirt. "Are you *crazy*? What were you gonna do, just *rape* me?"

"No!" I snapped, wanting to pimp slap the bitch. "I was hoping you'd be doing that to me!"

"*What?* My God! You have no class!" he shouted.

"*So what!* I want some ass!" I screamed.

"What man would want a woman who carries herself like this?" Ernest asked appallingly, both of his hands crossed prissily over his frail chest.

"Each and every goddamn one of them!" I yelled, my arms flying everywhere in exasperation. "What man *wouldn't* want me? I'm wearing a minidress that's about as flimsy as your *dick*, my black thong is made of lace, and I jacked you up and stroked you down on the dance floor all night long! I think you owe me an apology for severely leading me on."

"The only thing I owe you is a ride home," Ernest said as he rolled his eyes, flipped his hand up in my face, and switched his hips over toward the door. I'd never noticed that fluid catwalk thing before.

"Bottom line here," Ernest continued as he stood by the door with his hands on his hips, "is that you were cute, you were cool, and you liked good music. I thought you'd be fun to hang out with. It was just that simple. But I can't be bothered with all this mess," he went on, hands flying and fingers snapping everywhere. "I don't need all this drama in my life."

"Well, maybe you're right, girlfriend," I said, throwing on my shoes and grabbing my purse. It took me a while, but I was finally getting the picture. Ernest was a pantywaist.

"It ain't even like that, *girlfriend*," Ernest replied sarcastically as he smacked his lips and swiveled his neck.

"*Whateva!*" I laughed, suddenly not feeling so dejected after all. Ernest didn't want to be *with* me because he wanted to *be* me!

We walked to the car in silence. Ernest didn't say one word during the drive to my place. Lucky for me, I was still a little buzzed and didn't have to face the brutal reality of this ludicrous incident just yet. Ernest couldn't get me home fast enough.

"Thanks for the fun night," I quipped as he pulled up in front of my building. "Call me—maybe we can do it again sometime!"

"Honey, *please*," Ernest sighed, rolling his eyes harder than ever. Then he sped off before I'd barely even closed the car door.

"*Pussy*," I said to myself. It was the liquor talking.

Bottom Damn Line: Fuck a fence-straddling pansy who makes you feel like a manly reject.

II

I
Want
It
All

I want a man who's kind and understanding. Is that too
much to ask of a millionaire?

—Zsa Zsa Gabor

I Want It All

There are those of us who want to be successful. Who want nice things out of life. Who want to be happy. Who have dreams, set goals, work hard, and strive to achieve those goals. Eventually we do achieve them. Our mission has been accomplished. We look inside ourselves. We are proud. Our hearts are good. Our spirituality is strong. We look outside ourselves. Our careers are great. Our houses are magnificent. Our cars are luxurious. We look at ourselves. The diamonds in our ears are blinging. The clothes on our backs are designer. The portfolios in our hands are robust. We look next to ourselves. Something is missing. It is a mate.

We decide that companionship is in order. We must find someone to complete our powerful picture. During our search, we have to keep in mind that we have dreamed, set goals, and worked hard to achieve them. We are happy now. We are proud of ourselves. We have obtained nice things. So we want someone who has done the same. But that may be hard to find. We may end up settling for someone who wants to dream but can't fall asleep. Wants to move forward but can't find their feet. Desires the top but is stuck to the bottom. Lucky for them, our hearts are good. We've already gotten ours. And we don't mind courting them while they get theirs.

Then there are those of us who are sort of content with our lives. We may not necessarily be where we'd like to be, but we've come to terms with where we're at. We really don't feel like working toward our ultimate goals right now. And that's okay. Because we're just taking a break. We're comfortable in our meantime. Things could be better, but things could be worse. We could stand to go to church a little more, but we still read the Bible at home. We haven't found that dream job just yet, but our bills are still getting paid. Our car is not the latest model, but it still starts. We've managed to spice up last season's wardrobe with this season's accessories. Our bank accounts do not runneth over, but nevertheless, our checks are not bouncing.

So everything is okay. Not great. Not horrible. But okay. Yet something is definitely missing. It is a companion. It would be nice to meet someone. Someone who could contribute positively to our lives. Add some excitement. Offer some stability. Give us a boost. Introduce us to important people and take us to enticing places. Encourage us. Support us. Motivate us. Believe in us. And throw a little cash our way out of the kindness of their heart.

Then there are those of us whose shit just can't get right. We try, but to no avail. We've fallen, and we don't want to get up. We're tired. We're beaten. We're unlucky. We're discouraged. Opportunity runs when it sees us coming. Bill collectors ask how our families are doing. Holes and lint balls have invaded our played-out clothes. Our bank accounts are nonexistent. But we've worked hard to have two mandatory things on our side: good looks and good personalities.

For us, finding a mate is essential. Finding a rich mate is even more essential. We need someone to pick us up. To rescue us from our minuscule lives. Take us where we deserve to be. Teach us what we deserve to know. Give us what we deserve to have. Someone who wouldn't mind taking on a "project." Someone who would initially be satisfied with our good looks and good personalities, then willing to build on them. That would be our plan: to use what we've got to get what we want.

Status. Does it ever really matter when it's all said and done? Expectations. Is a situation sure to work just because they're all met? Destitution. Must someone save us from it or can we possibly save ourselves? Failure. Are we willing to accept a mate who knows nothing but? Loyalty. Can we judge those who deserve it and those who do not? Read on and explore how four men, ranging from low- to high-roller status, answered each of these questions for me.

Willy the Weed Smoker

Willy the Weed Smoker was an aspiring actor who was drunk and high all the damn time. His five all-time favorite things were alcohol, weed, fame, fortune, and sex. But the alcohol and weed definitely seemed to take precedence over all the others. It was ridiculous. And I'm not talking a little *sip-sip* here and a *puff-puff* there. I'm talking *here a sip, there a puff, everywhere a sip-puff. Dumb-ass Willy was a hype, E-I E-I OOOO*!

When Willy wasn't nursing a bottle he was clutching a blunt. When he wasn't clutching a blunt he was gripping a cigarette. I've even seen Willy nurse a bottle, clutch a blunt, and grip a cigarette all at the same time—at 7:00 A.M. As successful as he wanted to be, Willy was nothing but a thugged-out, unhappy, self-destructive man. Unfortunately, it took me way too long to figure that out.

I met Willy back in 1999. I'd just gotten out of a fucked-up relationship with a little-dick midget (you'll read about *him* later), and I was bitter and on the prowl. One night, a friend of mine took me to a local play that Willy was starring in. His performance had me nibbling on my nails and squirming in my seat. Willy was fine. He had flawless mahogany skin, short jet-black twists, a nice muscular build, and a wicked sense of humor. I admired his acting abilities. I knew no one who was even brave enough to pursue an acting career. My friend told me that she'd heard he was about to come up. I decided that I wanted to come up with him. I'd start by introducing myself to him after the play was over. But that didn't happen. Because he disappeared as soon as the curtain came down. I'd have to dust myself off and try again.

My second opportunity came. I met Willy's manager at a party the following weekend. He was old, bald-headed, pockmarked, and very flirtatious. I ignored his antics and expressed my interest in Willy. Lucky for me, this sleazy, forty-three-year-old ho-ass man was strung out on some eighteen-year-old slut who let men run trains on her and whatnot. So I didn't have to worry about him throwing salt in my plans. He eagerly agreed to hook me up and even clued me in to some of the things that Willy liked in women: good looks, good personality, intelligence, and being goal-oriented. I had all that, as far as I was concerned. But one thing he warned me about was Willy's regard for privacy. He suggested that I refrain from asking him about his personal life. I knew that would be a stretch for me, considering how nosy I was. But I decided that I could do it because Willy seemed worth it. His manager promised to give Willy my phone number and told me to expect a call sometime that week.

Willy called me a couple of days later, while I was working out. I recognized his voice immediately and felt an oblivious thrill—until he started talking in full sentences, that is. His words trickled out slow as hell, and he sounded dumb as hell. As I stepped off of my treadmill and struggled to catch my breath, Willy rambled on lethargically about his career, how everybody wanted to be down with him, how everybody wanted to blow up through him, and so on. By that time, my gut instinct was telling me to hang up the damn phone and go on about my business. But that would have been too much like right. So instead I continued the conversation and focused on how I was talking to a talented actor who would one day become a big star and take me to movie premieres and the Oscars.

But after conversing for about twenty more minutes, I couldn't deny the fact that Willy was a goddamn idiot. I finally came to my senses and drew the conversation to a close by saying, "Well, okay, it was nice talking to you. Maybe we'll meet sometime when we're both out or something." I thought that was good. I thought I was being smart and letting go of something that didn't seem right for me. Damn his aspirations and promising future, because he appeared to be a bumbling idiot. But then, contrary to his comatose attitude, Willy came back with an unexpected response.

"Well, what are you doing for lunch? Why don't you meet me somewhere so I can see you?" he suggested sluggishly.

Damn, I thought to myself. *Just say no, like Nancy Reagan said!* But then I remembered I was a Democrat.

"Okay," I replied. "What time do you want to meet?"

"Two o'clock?"

"Cool!" I said, and we made arrangements.

What the hell was I thinking? Why was I going to meet this inept moron? Why did I start unrealistically rationalizing with myself? I thought that maybe he'd be different in person. Maybe he was just tired from his hectic rehearsal and performance schedule. Think Oscars. Think premieres. Think of the time. It was 1:12 P.M. I had less than an hour to transform myself into a movie star's wife.

I dressed in all black like *The Omen*. My clingy tank dress was simple enough and did the trick. But on the way to the restaurant, I began having doubts. I prayed that I wouldn't end up like one of those dumb bitches in scary movies who fall during the chase. Deep down I knew I would. But I ignored it. I was too busy thinking Oscars. I was too busy thinking premieres.

I arrived at the restaurant first. I ordered something to drink and sat down at a table close to the door. I was fidgety as I waited impatiently for over thirty minutes, wiggling my foot and tugging at my dress the whole time. As soon as I contemplated leaving, Willy walked through the door. He was wearing a pale blue fitted shirt and dark gray pants. His muscular chest and arms were flexing. His twists were neatly slicked back. His diamond studs were icy. He was like a breath of fresh air. Until he got closer and I choked on his weed-laced aroma.

"Man! You're not what I expected," Willy proclaimed after I smiled and waved.

The compliment had me blushing like this was lunch with Will Smith, as opposed to Willy the Weed Smoker. "Well, what did you expect?" I gagged slightly.

"Not you," he gushed, eyes wide open.

Willy sat down across from me and stared at my breasts. He had my stomach trembling so much that I lost my appetite. So I just sat there as he ordered, then devoured his food. Afterward, he discussed several of his personal opinions and experiences with me. I was surprised. I'd been expecting a closed-off individual. But instead I'd gotten a man who didn't mind talking about his DUIs, his efforts to quit smoking and drinking, his desire to make it big, and his attempts to convert his corrupt friends into legitimate citizens. I must admit, I felt honored. Because for some ass-dumb reason, whenever men revealed their pitiful souls and exposed their pathetic, depressing lives to me, I melted like butta. I felt essential. So essential that I decided that Willy was an honest man with a good heart, good intentions, and good aspirations who deserved a chance.

After lunch, Willy invited me back to his place so that we could *talk* some more. I almost said no. But then I thought paparazzi. I thought red carpet. The combination urged me to say yes. So I went. When we arrived there, I realized that Willy lived with his mother. He was a struggling artist, so I let it slide.

Willy led me past a stuffy living room filled with old plaid furniture covered in thick plastic and shelves stocked with religious figurines. We walked down a hallway that had a huge picture of Mother Mary holding Baby Jesus hanging from the wall. We entered his bedroom. Willy plopped down on his wooden bed and threw me that come-hither look. I sat down on his weight-lifting bench instead, silently notifying him that there would be no penis between us. Willy looked baffled at first, then shook it off and began talking about college basketball.

As he babbled on, I looked around at all the boots, jerseys, and jeans he had thrown everywhere. Willy's bulky wooden dresser was lined with multiple brands of empty beer bottles, scattered ashes, colorful books of matches, and specks of blunt droppings. I got disgusted. But then I thought *Access Hollywood*. I thought *Entertainment Tonight*. I suddenly felt better.

After about two hours of video games, cigarettes, blunts, and beers, I decided that it was time to leave. Willy seemed disappointed as he grabbed his groin and got up to walk me to the door. He promised to call me the next day. I told him I'd be looking forward to it. For some strange reason, I was excited. Excited because I'd fooled myself into thinking that I was about to get with an almost-star. So excited that I called all of my girls as soon as I got home and told them about the afternoon. They were excited too. I accidentally skipped the part about the DUIs, the drinking, and the smoking.

The next day I sat by the phone and waited for Willy to call. He didn't. The day after that I sat by the phone and waited for Willy to call. He didn't. The third day, I broke down and called him. He wasn't home, so I left a message. Three days later he still hadn't called, and I was about to tear my hair out. Finally, after about two damn weeks, Willy called. I didn't know whether to jump up and down or cuss his ass out. After he invited me over, I decided to jump up and down.

When I arrived at Willy's apartment, he came to the door dressed in a dingy T-shirt, bleached-out doo-doo brown jogging pants, and one sock. He was clutching a beer bottle in one hand and a cigarette in the other. As I walked through the door, Willy leaned over and sluggishly brushed his lips against my cheek, then exhaled a beer-scented puff of air right in my face. I crinkled my nose in disgust and hoped that this wasn't his attempt at a kiss hello. As I reached out to warmly greet and embrace Willy the right way, he turned around and silently sauntered back toward his bedroom. Can you say *crunchy*? But then I thought bright lights. I thought *E! Fashion Review*. I got over it.

Willy had disappeared into his bedroom. I followed him. When I reached the doorway, he was leaning out of the window and sucking for dear life on a half-inch blunt. The cigarette that he'd carried to the front door was now propped in an ashtray on his dresser. His video game had been paused on the television screen. Clothes were strewn everywhere. After damn near igniting his lips and fingertips trying to inhale the very last drop of weed, Willy let out a yell. Then he flicked the remains out the window and fell invitingly onto the bed. I was still standing in the doorway, amazed by what I had just witnessed.

"Take off your clothes and come lay next to me," Willy said casually, rolling over and turning off the television. "Close the door and hit that light first." Then he began to strip.

I was stunned speechless. But Willy was now wearing nothing but his underwear. Tight black Calvin Kleins. My favorite. I liked what I saw. It had been a long time. His self-assured arrogance and bossiness was turning me on. So without saying another word I closed the door, hit the light, stripped down to my lacy lavender unmentionables, and slid into bed next to him.

As I lay there, perpetrating like I wasn't new to this thuggish type of aggressive, demanding behavior, Willy glided next to me and began biting my neck. "So, what did you get your degree in?" he grumbled, clawing his way toward the back of my bra.

Willy was so wrong for that weak-ass attempt at trying to sound interested. Like he really gave a fuck about my education. I doubt that he even heard my response, because by that time he was busy tugging at my panties. Before I knew it, the bull had been let out of the gate and the rodeo was about to begin.

Willy was good that first time. Good, but rehearsed. The sex was general and form-letterish. It was the type of sex that every random chick probably received. It didn't involve any real affection or intimacy. Willy's moves were mechanical, like he was acting in a porno movie (maybe he was—I didn't check the closets). But I knew not to expect much else from a hood rat who I'd just met.

After that day, my already unsteady relationship with Willy tumbled straight to hell. Drunken stupors, smoked-out sex sessions, and late-night phone calls were all I got from him. Our last-minute meetings were always scheduled during obscene hours. We never went anywhere. We just met at either his place or mine. I cram to understand how the so-called relationship lasted for as long as it did. I wasted so much time trying to do the undoable—change a man.

When Willy wouldn't change, I blamed his unacceptable behavior on all of his rejected auditions, weed smoking, and vodka drinking.

After a few months of this bullshit, I still hadn't earned the title of Willy's girlfriend. I didn't even want it, but by that time it was just the principle. Plus, when the day came that his career took a turn for the better, I had to have my position cemented for the sake of photos and interviews. But until that day came, Willy felt the need to tell anyone who was listening exactly where I stood, which was somewhere in special friend–land.

On one of the rare occasions when Willy and I when actually out together, he decided to stop by a friend's good-bye party. It was being thrown at some run-down lounge located in a horrendous neighborhood. The friend had been indicted and was being carted off to prison the following day to begin serving an extensive term. The charge was unknown to me.

As soon as we walked through the door, Willy ordered three shots of Hennessy and three bottles of beer. All for himself. Then, after he was good and drunk, he started ranting and raving about how everybody in the place was staring at him and how he gets tired of people sweating him everywhere he goes. I just played crazy and acted like I didn't know the idiot as I continued my conversation with the convict's girlfriend.

During our conversation, the convict's girlfriend referred to Willy as my boyfriend. I didn't correct her—not because I was trying to front, but because it was unnecessary. It would have thrown off the flow of the conversation. It was no big deal. We were well past her statement and on to another topic when Willy's drunk ass staggered in between our ripped up red vinyl barstools and leaned against me. I rolled my eyes and braced myself, figuring that he'd heard her and had a rebuttal.

"We not kickin' it like that, we just *coool*," Willy slurred loudly. "She my *girl*," he continued, shaking my shoulder like I was one of his boys. "But we ain't like that."

"Oh, okay," the convict's girlfriend stuttered, confused but not wanting any trouble. Willy then winked at me, ordered another round, and stumbled back over to the convict and the rest of their friends.

Why am I here? I asked myself. I could have shot Willy dead for embarrassing me like that. I knew I was too good to be getting played by a broke-ass, fucked-up, wanna-be-but-ain't-never-gonna-be-famous, hype-ass loser. But you know me. I just sat my dumb ass right there and acted like I didn't even hear him, let alone care. 'Cuz Willy was gonna come up. He was gonna *be* somebody. And I was gonna be right there with him. Because I believed in him. Reminds me of one of my favorite old tunes: "Everybody Plays The Fool."

And a fool I was. As our relationship continued, Willy continued to play me. As he continued to play me, I continued to support him. Like the time when he was supposedly deathly ill and called to tell me about it. I offered to bring him some food and medicine. He immediately accepted. When I got to his apartment, he went straight into the kitchen and made the tea, took the medicine, and ate the food that I'd delivered without even looking at me. A hello or thank you would have been good enough. But I didn't trip. I just sat my stupid ass in the corner and watched, glad to be of some assistance.

After he'd gotten himself together, Willy finally called me over to thank me properly. He thanked the hell outta me, and then we quietly cuddled and watched television. It was the type of calm, tranquil circumstance we rarely experienced. So I savored every moment. Then the telephone rang. It interrupted my momentary bliss. Needless to say, I was quite pissed. But I figured that since we were having such a wonderful time, Willy would let the voice mail pick up. Contrary to my idiotic assumption, he jumped up and almost knocked me to the floor trying to get to the phone.

Willy glanced at the caller ID, grabbed the phone, and feverishly shouted, "Hey, Puss 'n Boots!"

Can you say *stunned*? My mouth fell open and my eyes squinted. I turned away so that Willy wouldn't see my outraged expression.

"You're *here*?! Well, I'm getting ready to run out, but why don't you just come by and wait for me to get back? You *know* you got it like that . . ."

My head swiveled around at lightning speed. I glared at Willy. If looks could kill, he'd be one dead mutha. He glanced at me and quickly turned away, not wanting to die before he got to fuck Miss Puss 'n Boots. He actually sat there and made plans with her right in my face. Then he hung up the phone and acted as if nothing had happened. Therefore, I did too, with my dumb ass. After all, if I ever wanted to make this man settle down, fall in love, and commit to me, I had to appear cool and unfazed by mess like this, right? I had to get used to groupies and back-burners and bullshit, right?

Wrong. I eventually got myself together and got fed up with Willy's mess. It took long enough, but I made it there. I could no longer stomach our stagnant situation and his fictitious future. One night I went to his house on a mission. I was ready to tell him it was over. "I need and deserve more," I declared as soon as I got there.

But then I began to choke up during my speech. Suddenly I realized that I only *sort of* meant what I was saying. Yes, I did need and deserve more, but I wanted Willy to give me more. Not walk away. But it didn't matter. Because walk away he did. The watery-eyed, emotional explanation Willy gave me had me going. He told me that he cared, but couldn't settle down because of his career.

I told him that I made him happy.

He told me that success would make him happier.

I was enraged and told him to kiss my ass.

He flipped me over and did.

I pushed him off me and walked out. For good.

Willy and I don't talk anymore. I've relapsed now and then (I called and wrote him a couple of times), but luckily for me, he never responded. One night I saw him at a club and he ran up and hugged me like we'd fought in the war together and I'd saved his life. I pushed him off me and kept on walking. I couldn't even look him in the eye. After that incident we stopped speaking to each other altogether.

Oh, wait. Did I mention the time Willy made me take him to his drug dealer's house at 4:45 in the morning? He purchased several dime bags through the dealer's bedroom window. I just couldn't handle that. When he got back in the car I called him a crackhead, which really hurt his little feelings. Oh, well. He shouldn't have referred to some bitch as Puss 'n Boots in front of me.

Bottom Damn Line: Fuck a thugged-out crackhead who's "finna" come up.

Leroy the Loser-Ass Liar

Leroy's Wish List
I wish I was a baller,
I wish I could get paid
To play ball in the NBA,
And get my lying ass laid.

Damn the fact
That I'm real fat
And have no fucking skills;
I'll be a star,
Drive a nice car,
And feast on baller meals.

If only I'd get chose,
Then I could get on hos.
I'd be all in the media,
Dressed in designer clothes.

But till the day
That I can say,
I play ball in the NBA,
I'll keep on lying
And keep on trying
To find my broke-ass way.

Leroy was such a loser. And he was such a liar. Bottom line: Leroy was *such* a loser-ass liar. He wanted to play ball in the NBA. *Bad.* But he couldn't make it. He tried and he tried, but the boy just couldn't make it. He played hard in high school and college and couldn't make it. He went to basketball camps and couldn't make it. He played in local tournaments and couldn't make it. He hung out with NBA players and couldn't make it. He supposedly got signed with a fourth rate agent and couldn't make it. He supposedly played overseas and couldn't make it. But he wouldn't give up. He was either going to make it to the NBA or he was going to die trying.

Leroy and I met several years ago through an old classmate of mine. At six foot seven, Leroy must have weighed well over three hundred pounds (initially that was all muscle). He was so tall that I never really looked up at him. The pain in my neck was too excruciating when I tried. So I can't remember exactly what he looked like. He wasn't much to write home about, though. Just big and brown. But his personality made up for all that. Leroy was funny as hell. He could crack a good joke and do the best imitations. Maybe he should have pursued a career in comedy. He damn sure would have been more successful with that than trying to do the pro-basketball thing.

Leroy was such a fucking liar it was unbearable. Just ridiculous. He lied about *everything*. The first lie was about his birthday. The summer that we met, Leroy told me he was twenty-two-years old (two years younger than me at the time), and that his birthday was in August. He claimed he was leaving to go play ball in Paris that fall (where he'd supposedly signed a $10 million contract) and wanted to hang out with me before he left. When he started suggesting how he'd sponsor my trips to Paris so that I could visit him and consider moving there, my interest really sparked. After all, we were becoming fast friends and enjoying each other's company. We had a lot in common. Music, movies, ambition, drive—it was all there. And what girl in her right mind with nothing to lose would pass up moving to Paris to be with a millionaire and live happily ever after? I damn sure wouldn't.

So I decided to start playing my cards right with his birthday. I'd make it a memorable one. I searched all over the place for his favorite movies and CDs so that he could take them to Paris. I made dinner reservations at one of the finest restaurants in town. I put together a beautiful outfit to wear. Then I went to the store to buy wrapping paper and candles for the cake I was planning to bake for him.

As I perused the aisles of the store, one of our mutual friends saw me, said hello, and asked what I was up to. I told her today was Leroy's twenty-third birthday and that I was picking up some things for him. She looked at me like I was crazy and told me Leroy's birthday was in March and that he'd be turning nineteen. I looked at her like *she* was crazy and insisted that she must be mistaken. Leroy was of age and he was not a liar. She told me she was going to check into his claim and inform me of the results. I told her to do what she liked, walked off, and didn't think anything else about it.

That night, Leroy and I ate steak and lobster and drank

way too much merlot. I paid the bill, knowing I couldn't afford it but also knowing that I'd be reimbursed a hundred times over in the future. After dinner, I took Leroy back to my place for dessert. His beautifully wrapped gifts and three-layer chocolate cake were waiting for him as soon as he walked through the door. Leroy was so touched. He grabbed me, gave me a big hug, then kissed me right on the lips. I let him get away with it since he'd be leaving for another country and I'd be joining him soon. We ate cake, watched some of the movies I'd bought for him, and cuddled just a bit. There would be no throw-down at the ho-down until my trip to Paris. I couldn't play myself.

The story that my friend had told me in the store earlier that day ran through my mind periodically, but I chose to ignore it. Leroy and I were having a great time together. We were embarking on a friendship that would probably lead to much more. Plus, he had no reason to lie to me.

Leroy left for Paris a few weeks later. He said he'd send for me as soon as possible. He said he'd call just as soon as he got there. And he did. I was thrilled. I didn't care that it was the middle of the night and I had to be up for work in a few hours. I was just glad to hear his voice. I was glad he'd made it. I was glad he hadn't forgotten about me. The women of Paris hadn't taken over. The $10 million contract hadn't gone to his head. Leroy still wanted me there. He was asking how soon I could come. He told me how beautiful every-thing was. He told me how fabulous his house was. I jokingly told him I'd turn in my letter of resignation that same day. I didn't tell him I was really serious.

Leroy and I talked for over three hours. I was concerned about the phone bill, but he didn't care. He could afford it now. Before we hung up, Leroy promised to send me some pictures and goodies. I hoped they'd all be designer and expensive. He asked if I was still interested in moving there with him. I told him yes. He asked if I could come and visit within the next couple of weeks. I told him yes, even though I had no vacation time left at work. My job no longer mattered. Nothing mattered. I was moving to Paris to live a glamorous life with a millionaire. I would scream, "How you like me now?" from the rooftop and tell everybody to kiss my ass, 'cuz I'd made it and they hadn't. I silently thanked Leroy for providing my story with a fairy-tale ending. Leroy told me to be looking out for his package, and we said good-bye.

I got up and pirouetted to the bathroom. It was time to go to work, and I didn't care that I'd gotten no sleep. I wouldn't be staying anyway. I'd compose my resignation letter before I left home, hand deliver it to my boss, then walk the fuck out. She always treated me like shit anyway, with her big fat Linda Tripp–looking ass. Now I'd finally be able to give her a taste of her own shit. As a matter of fact, damn a hand delivery. I'd fax the letter to the bitch. And I'd tell her exactly why I was quitting. I'd inform her that I was moving to Paris, which was one of her favorite places, to marry a millionaire and live happily ever after. Rather than *Sincerely*, I'd sign off with *Fuck you* and call it a damn day.

I imagined visiting spas and spending Leroy's money and dining in cafés all throughout Paris. I imagined attending his basketball games in Chanel suits. I flushed the toilet and walked back into my bedroom. I turned the light on. I checked the caller ID to see what had come up when Leroy called. I was expecting to see *Unavailable* or *Private*. What I actually saw was *Holiday Inn Express*. Huh?

Now I was confused. There must have been some mistake. Leroy had called me from his fabulous house in Paris, not some Holiday Inn Express that was obviously somewhere within the United States. I dialed the phone number that was displayed below the hotel name. A woman answered and said, "Holiday Inn Express, how may I help you?" I asked what state she was in. She said Mississippi. I asked for Leroy Johnson's room. I was connected immediately. Leroy answered the phone. I hung right up without saying a word. I had no time to talk or scream or curse because I had to hurry up and get ready for work before I was late.

When I got to the office I felt as if I'd contracted walking pneumonia. I had a fever. I had chills. I was turning blue. My head ached. My eyes were red and glassy from lack of sleep and disappointment. I looked like a crackhead going through withdrawal. My dream had been deferred, and I couldn't get over it. I rocked back and forth in my chair like a psychopath. I longed for a blanket. My clothes didn't match. My blouse was apple green and my skirt was fiery red. I didn't know what my shoes looked like. I couldn't look that far down because my head was pounding too hard. Important clients were coming into the office that day. My presentation was ready, but I wasn't. My evil boss offered to step in and present for me if I wanted to go home. I told her I thought I was coming down with a stomach flu and strep throat, which would mean

I could stay out of the office for the rest of the week. She got my purse and jacket for me and pushed me into the elevator so that she wouldn't get sick or be embarrassed when the clients arrived. I didn't care. Nothing mattered. My future had collapsed right before my very eyes.

Leroy wouldn't stop calling me. I wouldn't answer the phone. He was no longer calling from the Holiday Inn Express. He was now calling from Mississippi State University. I couldn't bring myself to say one word to him. The mere thought induced mental and physical illness. I had to get better and move on. The friend I'd seen in the store the day of his pseudobirthday called. She knew Leroy had told me he was in Paris. She confirmed that he was in Mississippi starting his sophomore year of college. She confirmed that he wasn't yet nineteen-years old. She confirmed that his birthday was in March. She confirmed that his mediocre talent would never carry him to a professional basketball career. My watering mouth confirmed that I was about to vomit. I hung up in her face.

Two years passed. Leroy and I had no contact whatsoever. One night when I was out at a club, I saw this guy who I used to kind of date. I now hated him. The only reasons I had dealt with his ignorant, inarticulate, exaggerating ass was because he gave me money, was very popular, and spoke very highly of me in the street. He came up and kissed my cheek hello. I asked how he was doing. He said he was good and asked if I'd spoken to my boy Leroy. I'd had no idea that he knew Leroy, or that he knew that I knew Leroy, for that matter. I was protesting and trying to tell him that I wasn't cool with Leroy when he interrupted and told me that Leroy was back in town.

"From Mississippi?" I asked.

"No, from Spain," he responded.

"*Spain?* I thought he was at school in Mississippi."

"Hell naw! Leroy's been playing ball in Spain for the past year and a half. He was only in Mississippi for a minute before his agent found him a spot on Spain's team," he insisted.

"Well, I don't know about all that," I said skeptically. I knew good and damn well that Leroy hadn't been in Spain. He'd fooled not just me but everydamnbody else, too.

"Straight up! My cousin who plays in Japan played Spain a few months ago. He told me that Leroy was on the team."

My ears perked up. This was no lie. Leroy had really made it. I wouldn't have minded living in Spain. Why had he lied before? Why hadn't he called to tell me? But he *had* called. I'd just refused to talk to him. Maybe I'd forgive him now.

"Well, where is he staying?" I asked anxiously.

"He's at his mother's house. I don't know how long he's going to be in town, though."

"Thanks for the info. It was good seeing you," I said, rushing toward the exit. I had to get home. I had to find out if Leroy had called me and if I still had the opportunity to resign from my job. Spain wasn't as good as Paris, but I could adjust. Millions of dollars could make me adjust to damn near anything.

Sure enough, Leroy had left me a message. He said he

missed me. He said he didn't understand why we hadn't talked in so long. He wanted to make sure we were still cool. He left the number to his mother's house. I called there immediately.

"Hey, stranger," Leroy said.

"Hey," I replied. I hadn't planned what I would say to him. But our conversations had always flowed easily. So I had no trouble falling right back in with him.

"Where you been?" he asked.

"Working," I said.

"Are we still cool?" he asked.

"Of course," I replied quickly, not wanting to bring up his past lies for fear that it would ruin our possible future.

"Well, I wondered, because you never returned my calls. I left Paris and went to Spain for a better position on their team and more money. I was looking forward to you being there with me."

"You know, I had so much going on around that time," I lied, turning on my computer and pulling up my resignation-letter template. "But all that's behind us now. When are you going back?"

"I'm not," he replied. "I got cut. So I'm looking for a spot either in the NBA, in another country, or, push come to shove, on an NBA practice team. My agent thinks my chances are good for the NBA. Overseas should be no problem, and the practice team would be a last resort. If I end up on a practice team, I'll play with the actual players and hopefully secure a spot on the team. But I'll still be considered a *part* of the team. Plus, I'll make somewhere in the millions just like them, and travel with them, too. So whichever route I take, I'll be straight."

I closed out my resignation-letter template as uncertainty loomed overhead. My future still looked too murky for me to make any immediate decisions. I would have to wait and see where this was going before I made any big moves.

"What are you doing right now?" Leroy asked.

"Nothing," I said, glancing at the clock. It was after two in the morning.

"Well, can I stop by? My boy is coming that way and I haven't seen you in so long I forgot what you look like!"

"Okay." I shrugged, ignoring the clock and suddenly anxious to see Leroy the so-called baller again.

When Leroy arrived, he looked immaculate. Designer gear from head to toe. Clean-cut, nice jewelry, and a smile that assured me he was ecstatic to see me. I was still in there. None of those Spanish broads had faded me. He still wanted me. I pushed his lies out of my head and focused on the from here on out.

Leroy and I talked, laughed, watched one of our favorite movies, tickled each another in the bed, and played footsie. But I still couldn't give him none. I couldn't play myself. I had to keep his desire on fire. I had to keep his respect in effect. That way, when the NBA came calling, I would be able to come running like I was the one being drafted.

Leroy spent the night. I put secure underwear on underneath my pajamas so that he wouldn't get any ideas. I didn't get any sleep because his bigness took up the whole damn bed. The sun rose and I was successful in my quest to remain abstinent. I deserved a gold medal, because I had actually been going through a mini-drought. One of Leroy's boys paged him and said he was coming to pick him up. I wondered why Leroy hadn't driven his own car, which damn sure should have been a Mercedes or something, but I didn't ask because I didn't want any trouble.

Leroy left, and I waited. And I waited. And I waited. Still no word from the NBA or a team overseas. Leroy went away to a couple of basketball camps, but as my father said, if you ain't playing like Shaq, you ain't getting picked by a team through a camp.

A few months passed. Still no word. Leroy was getting idle. His muscle was turning to fat. His clothes were getting too tight. He thought he'd have to resort to a practice team that year. But that was impossible. Because the type of practice team that Leroy had described to me didn't exist in the NBA. I found that one out through my father, too. Leroy was up to his old tricks again. He was lying again. As it happened, Leroy had never played ball in Spain. His boy had. Leroy had moved there to see if he could ride on his boy's coattails and grab an opportunity. He couldn't. So he'd come back to town with his dejected tail tucked between the crack of his fat ass. Leroy was dead broke. He had no money. He had no car. He had no pro-basketball-playing future. He was a farce, a fraud, a scrub, a pool of lard biting off of everyone else's success. He had no agent. He had nothing but some old-ass, bench-warming alumni basketball players from Mississippi State trying to hook him up with some low-budget bullshit.

I'd had it. I erased Leroy from my life forever. He stalked me for a while, but to no avail. I couldn't take the lies any longer. He couldn't rescue me. He couldn't rescue himself. So I didn't answer the calls that he placed all day, everyday. I told my doorman I wasn't home when Leroy came to see me. I told my friends to tell Leroy that I'd moved out of the country. He is now a blubbery, lying-ass loser slob who does nothing and drives around in his grandmother's van, lives off his mother, and still wants to make it to the goddamn NBA. Not gonna happen. With no backup plan, his future looks mighty bleak. Lucky for me, his forecast predicts no sunshine of mine whatsoever.

> **Bottom Damn Line:** Fuck a fake-ass slam-dunker
> Who's as fat as Archie Bunker,
> Who will never play ball pro,
> 'Cuz he's lukewarm, big, and slow.

Warren the So-Called Wonder

arren was the man I thought I would marry. The one who walked into my life, turned down the lights, and lit a candle. The one who reminded me that miracles really do happen. That dreams really do come true. That fantasies really do become realities. And in the end, that the devil really works just as hard as the Lord.

When I met Warren, nothing was really going my way. I was working a fucked-up, go-fetch-me-some-coffee type of job. I had been pursuing a singing career on the low for a long while and still hadn't gotten signed. I couldn't buy a date. My money was too funny. I felt fat. I felt stagnant. I was trying to fill my half-empty glass but couldn't find no water.

Then, as if my life wasn't ignorant enough, the engine in my car blew out. I had no ends to get it fixed. I had no other way to get around. So I did the unthinkable. I had a pharmaceutical street salesman from around the way flip some money for me. He did his thing and gave me back double what I'd given him.

I deposited the hustled duckets in my bank account. I had to wait three weeks for an appointment to get the engine transplant. The only dealership able to perform the operation was far, far away. I had to have the car towed there and wait for hours. After the far, far away dealership finally fixed the car, they wouldn't take my check. I had no credit card.

They had no loaner car. I ended up having to call my mommy and daddy and ask them to pick me up. I would have to go all the way back out to the far, far away dealership the next day to fetch my car. I felt extremely shitty.

I waited two hours for my parents to arrive. The far, far away dealership eventually closed. I had to sit outside in the blue-black night and wait in the parking lot. My cell phone wouldn't dial out, so I couldn't even phone a friend. Ma and Pa eventually arrived. I was thankful yet pissed, freezing yet musty, cranky and exhausted and very ready to go home. But they had to stop and get gas. They had to put air in the tires. They had to get something to eat. They had to buy some fuses. They started arguing. By the time we pulled into the drugstore parking lot I was ready to jump in front of a moving vehicle and end it all. But instead I decided to go inside and buy my funky ass some deodorant.

As I walked through the store, I held my arms close against my body so not to offend anyone. When I turned down the snack aisle, an extreme cutie was bestowed upon me. He was rummaging through potato-chip bags. His hair was thick and unruly. His skin was light tan and silky smooth. His long, lush lashes surrounded slanted brown eyes. His body was out of sight. He was looking real right. Even though I wasn't, I walked past anyway just to get a better look. I got close. He turned around. Well, what do you know. It was Warren, a guy who an ex-friend of mine had been in love with back in the day. He'd never given her any play. Maybe he'd give me some. My moldy ass could be the one. After taking a few moments to convince myself I didn't look *that* damn bad, I decided to go over and speak.

"Hi, Warren?" I smiled, my arms stiff and still and my nails scraping nervously against my cuticles.

"Yes?" he turned and smiled back, staring at me blankly with no clue as to who the hell I was. I stood there, allowing him the opportunity to run through his mental archive and check his memory. The longer I waited, the louder the silence became. The louder the silence became, the faster his smile faded. The faster his smile faded, the sweatier my underarms became. I wanted to turn around and flee. But it was too late for that. So all my rambunctious ass could do was pray that he couldn't smell me, then stumble and bumble my way through this ordeal.

"Yeah, ahh, I met you a few years ago?" I hinted.

He was still silent.

"During college?"

He stared at me as if I were disturbed.

"Through Tricia?"

He started shuffling and fidgeting and getting uncomfortable.

"I think she was a friend's little sister?"

He reached for his cell phone to call the police.

"Sooo, how are you?" I asked desperately. It was my final attempt before being handcuffed and charged with stalking and harassment. A cold, dejected drop of perspiration fell from my right armpit and rolled down my love handle. It represented the tear of stupidity that wanted to fall from my eye.

"Ohh, yeah, I remember now!" Warren said, suddenly brightening up. "I'm sorry—it's been a long day. What's up? You're looking good!"

The sudden burst of energy surged from his lips to my pulse. My heartbeat rocked my body back and forth. My eyes went blind from that bright, shiny smile. My palms went dry. My panties went wet. It was all good now.

"Oh, I haven't been up to much," I told Warren. "What about you?"

"Just working hard," he replied modestly, staring down at the floor. It was my turn now.

"I've been working hard, too." Then I decided to let my one and only strong, healthy cat out the bag. "Actually, I was out in L.A. a few months ago visiting with One Time Records. They're considering signing me. So I've been working on some songs and waiting to hear back from them."

"Really? That's tight!" Warren proclaimed. "I'm a manager and I've got some connections over at One Time. Who do you know there?"

As I rattled off my contacts, I just knew this was it. I'd found my creative soul mate. Look out, Bobby and Whitney *and* Will and Jada. There was about to be a new tag team in town. I told Warren we needed to hook up since I didn't have a manager. He agreed. I told him I had an outstanding demo tape. He told me he'd love to hear it. I suggested we exchange information. He suggested we do dinner. I told him I'd love to. He gave me his number and said he'd call later that week. My mother walked over and started sweating me to leave. I introduced her to Warren. I could tell she loved him. The hardest part of our relationship was already out of the way. Warren and I said our good-byes. I walked to the front of the store to pay for my deodorant. I looked back as I pulled money out of my wallet to see what Warren was doing. He was staring at me. He looked away fast when he saw me look over. I smiled at his cuteness.

Warren called me two days later. He invited me out to dinner that weekend. We ended up talking for over two hours. We discussed our caviar dreams and champagne wishes. We both wanted to make it big in the entertainment business. He ultimately wanted to own a production company. I ultimately wanted to own a record label. The sky was the limit for the both of us. We could ascend on clouds and float on stars together. Warren begged me not to forget to bring my demo tape to dinner. I promised him I wouldn't. He suggested we meet at the restaurant since he'd be coming from a business meeting across town. I told him that was fine and I was looking forward to it. He was too. We bid adieu.

Warren called me Saturday afternoon to confirm dinner. We talked for an hour and a half just because. He asked if I believed in love at first sight. I told him yes. I asked if he believed in love at first sight. He said yes. I wondered if he knew the first sight of him in the store had me smitten. I hoped his first sight of me in the store had him smitten too. Warren told me he was ready to settle down and start a family. I told him I was too. I hoped he wanted to start a family with me. I damn sure wanted to start a family with him. He told me he couldn't wait to see me. I told him I couldn't wait to see him. He told me he had to get ready and head out for his meeting. I wanted to tell him to get ready to head down the aisle. But instead I said good-bye and began preparing for our date.

I had to look as good as possible, considering Warren's previous encounter with my hygiene and appearance. I would soak in the tub, shave under my arms, use plenty of deodorant, and spray on refreshing perfume. I would wear my honey-colored butter-leather dress and tall leather boots to match. I would take my time when curling my hair so that it would look bouncy, silky, and perfect. I would apply a ton of subtle, neutral makeup so that my skin would glow flawlessly. I would be charming and appealing and alluring throughout the date. I would front when it was over and convince both Warren and myself that it was entirely too early in the relationship for him to come inside. After all, I knew this was it. So I had to take it slow and do it right.

Getting perfect took longer than I'd thought it would. I was running late and drove to the restaurant entirely too fast. I sucked on mints the whole way there to keep my dry mouth and throat moist and fresh. Even though the heat in my car was on full blast, my hands were rattling and my teeth were chattering. I arrived fifteen minutes late and pulled into the parking lot. I did a quick once-over in the rearview mirror before getting out of my car. I gripped my purse until my knuckles turned to five lumps of sugar. I struggled to control my jittery knees.

Entering the restaurant, I was shaky as hell and happy as hell, all at the same time. I reflected on how it had taken a lotta damn frogs to get me to my prince. I reflected on how it had taken a lotta damn hustling to get me to my record deal. The chill of my success was in the air. It cooled my skin and fanned my soul. I had made it. This was what it felt like at the top. And somebody had lied, because it damn sure didn't feel the least bit lonely.

The plush, dimly lit restaurant was packed. Everyone turned and stared as I moved through the crowd and searched for Warren. I practiced stardom by looking no one in the eye and maintaining an air of rushed, busy importance. I had no time for autographs and conversation. I had to find my manager/husband so that we could discuss business/pleasure. Time was money. Mine would no longer be funny. I was about to be a singing sensation. My starved ass hoped we had a reservation.

I found Warren standing in the back of the waiting area. He looked even better than before. Thank God I did, too. I smiled and went to hug him, but he took a step back and held out his hand instead. I hesitated crunchily, then shook his hand. A tall, bald, bifocaled guy standing next to him smiled at me. I raised my eyebrows in acknowledgment, then turned around, amazed by this fool's bold flirtation. He could see that I was with someone. The nerve of him. I hoped that Warren's conservatively cordial ass had peeped his behavior and was prepared to check him if necessary.

"So, how are you, Warren?" I purred, shaking off the residue that his distant greeting had left on me.

"Good, good." He yawned, leaning back against the wall. "Just a little tired. I had a lot going on today."

"Tell me about it," I sighed, knowing good and damn well my day had been filled with stapling papers and answering phones. But I was about to get signed to a big record label. I had to act important. The guy next to Warren was still staring and smiling at me. I was getting irritated and uncomfortable. He was being so obvious and rude.

"Oh, I'm sorry. I'm being rude," Warren said. "This is my assistant, Simon."

Warren pointed at the grinning weirdo who had been staring at me. They were together. I was confused. What the hell was *he* doing here? I started getting mad. I wanted to kick Warren in his fucking neck. I wanted to beat him in his burly chest. Only a pantywaist would bring his buddy on a date. I wanted to turn around and walk out.

"It's nice to meet you." Simon grinned even harder.

"Likewise," I muttered through clenched teeth. Then I excused myself and darted off to the bathroom. Once inside, I looked in the mirror and almost cried. I tried to understand why this cock-blocking, third-wheeling psycho was there. Was Warren afraid of me? Was he gay? Was this strictly business? A million possibilities ran though my mind. I wanted to climb out the window and escape this bullshit. I had thought this was *it*. But *it* was no longer what *it* was supposed to be. Business was supposed to be the breakthrough to pleasure. I was supposed to be a love-struck hunter, killing two birds with one stone. But instead I was a rockless fool, staring at an empty sky.

Before leaving the bathroom I glanced in the mirror and took stock. I looked appealing. I smelled delicious. I made a decision. I would not waste this night. I would give Warren a chance before pulling the plug. Maybe Simon had been at the meeting with Warren earlier and had gotten stuck with him. Maybe Warren had been running late for our date and had had no other choice but to bring him. Maybe it was good that Simon had tagged along. Maybe he would think I was great and encourage Warren to scoop up a good catch like me. Yeah, that's what would happen. I took a deep breath. I was proud of myself. I had just turned my sour attitude into sweet, lemony acceptance. I squared my shoulders. I left my meeting in the ladies' room to embark on my new mission.

When I reapproached Warren and Simon, they told me our table was ready. The host led the way. I snatched glances from diners' eyes on the way there. Simon definitely seemed to notice, but Warren paid no attention. He was in denial. He didn't want to face the fact that everyone either wanted or envied his future wife.

We arrived at the table. I was curious to see what the seating arrangement would be. Warren and Simon revealed it quickly: they sat next to each other on one side of the table while I sat on the other side, across from Warren. I couldn't decide whether this was a datelike seating arrangement for Warren and me or more of a business thing. Usually couples sat across from each other on dates, right? So that was a good thing. But Simon was sitting right next to Warren, which meant they would be close enough to touch each other and stuff, which was a bad thing. Shouldn't Warren have sat next to me so that *we* could touch each other and stuff? Or was the across-the-table date thing good enough? I couldn't decide. There were too many dents in every theory. So I came up with a new one: Simon should have stayed his goofy ass at home.

The three of us ordered dinner. Then Simon asked what I did for a living. I opted to tell him about my demo tape and potential contract with One Time Records, as opposed to my bullshit coffee-brewing, paper-stapling office job. He got excited as hell. I thought that was sweet as hell. But I was careful not to give Simon the wrong impression. He would be stickin' no dick in. I was all about Warren. But was he all about me? If he was, then why had he brought Simon Tag-along?

I forced myself to stop worrying about it and have a good time. And I did. Interesting conversation seasoned our dinner with much fun and laughter. We talked music. We talked sports. We talked movies. We talked Hollywood gossip. We talked hometown gossip. Warren told me I'd better eat all of my vegetables. I thought that was so cute. It meant he'd be a good father to our children.

During dessert, Warren demanded that I hand over my demo tape. He said he was eager to hear it and didn't want to leave the restaurant without it. I held it over the table. He reached out and pressed his fingers against mine, then slid the tape out of my hand. Our eyes converged. My breathing ceased. I couldn't look away. Neither could he. Simon was no longer there. Warren and I were submersed in an enchanting moment. I didn't want it to end. Life felt good right there. Warren's cell phone rang. The spell was broken. I wanted to climb onto the roof and jump.

Warren answered his phone. I glared at him for succumbing to the interruption. I glared at my phone and cursed all of my trifling girls who were supposed to call me during dinner to make me look important. I began to talk to Simon. Fuck Warren and his phone call. Simon cracked a good joke. I started laughing. Then his cell phone rang. He answered it. Fuck him, too.

I was sitting among two very important people. I felt isolated and embarrassed. I looked around to see if anyone was snickering at me. They weren't. If they were, it would have been the least of my concerns, because Warren had just told whoever was on the other end of his phone that he was at a business meeting. A *business meeting*? This was no goddamn business meeting! This was a bona fide date that he'd accidentally brought Simon Tag-along on, wasn't it?

The server brought the bill over to the table. Warren paid it. Simon paid the tip. I thanked both of them. The three of us got up and left the restaurant. Warren walked me to my car while Simon went to look in a store window. I silently thanked him for giving us some time alone. Warren told me he wanted to stop by and see my place but couldn't because he had to pick up some things at a client's house. He was going out of town the following week and asked if we could get together the weekend he returned. I told him yes. He said he couldn't wait to play my demo and listen to my beautiful voice flow through his speakers. I rose two feet above the ground and thanked him kindly. He leaned in as if he was going to kiss me. I closed my eyes and puckered up. I heard the clicking of hard-soled shoes approaching. I opened my eyes.

Simon Tag-along was back. My puckered lips recoiled. My zealous heart deflated.

Warren turned and looked at Simon. Then he turned back and gave me a big, tight hug instead of a soft, juicy kiss. I wanted to stab Simon in the neck but smiled in his face instead. At least I now had something to smile about. I knew I had been on a date. I knew Warren was interested in more than my demo tape and contract. I might have been greeted with a weak ass handshake, but I was leaving with a nice, warm hug.

After Warren released me from the cozy embrace, Simon came up and hugged me too. I thought that was sweet. But I wrapped only one arm around him and patted his back lightly. Had to remind him there would be no dippin' the dick in.

Warren opened my car door for me and made sure I got in okay. I thanked him. He told me he would call as soon as he got back in town. I told him I was looking forward to it and to be careful. I wanted to tell him to come home with me. But instead I stayed in a potential's place, waved good-bye, and drove off.

I gripped the steering wheel with both hands and bobbed and weaved in my seat the whole way home. I knew Warren and Simon were probably listening to my tape at that very moment. I was anxious to know what they thought. If only I were a fly on the dashboard. I became the next best thing. I popped a copy of my demo tape into the cassette player and pretended I was Warren. I pressed "play." I listened to my rendition of Anita Baker's "Been So Long" through Warren's ears. I decided that I wanted to marry this songstress through Warren's mind.

Two weeks later, Warren hadn't called. He'd been back in town for well over a week. I'd actually thought he'd call the night we'd had dinner to tell me that he loved my demo. When he didn't, I'd thought he'd call the next day. When he hadn't, I'd thought he'd call while traveling. When he hadn't, I'd definitely thought he'd call when he got back to tell me he had talked to his people at One Time Records and was pushing to get me signed. After all, he was almost my manager/future husband, wasn't he?

After three more days of impatient patience, I broke down and called Warren on his cell phone. He sounded quite happy to hear from me. It gave me hope. I asked how come he hadn't called when he'd gotten back in town. He claimed he'd had to stop over in L.A. and had just gotten back. I waited on the edge of my seat for him to tell me he'd convinced his homeys at One Time to sign me immediately. I fell off the edge of my seat when he instead asked if I'd heard anything. I told him no. I climbed back up into my seat and explained that I had no clout and needed an insider to get the process going and the contracts flowing. I waited on the edge of my seat again for him to tell me that he'd make some calls. I fell off again when he told me to keep my head up and keep him posted. Then he said his phone battery was running out and that he'd call me when he got home. I said okay and hung up. I was tired of falling down and getting hurt, so I laid my ass out on the floor and vowed to stay there until he called back. Needless to say, I woke up the next morning in that exact same spot.

Three weeks passed. No word from Warren. I guess he was still on his way home. We were no longer Whitney and Bobby or Will and Jada. We were now Bruce and Demi, Halle and Eric. The party was over. The wedding bells had cracked. The star-power couple had left the building (through separate exits). My bad-luck spell was back in effect and bigger than ever.

Then the unthinkable happened. One Time Records called and told me they were in the final stages of making a decision. They said things were looking good. They promised to get back to me by the end of the week. I hung up the phone and thought about how the next time Warren heard from me, it would be through a microphone onstage at the Grammys. I would win Best New Artist. My album would go forty times platinum. Warren's name would be nowhere in my acceptance speech. Hot vapors of regret would singe his spine. Vicious bites of grief would nip his ears. Green pricks of envy would stab his heart.

The phone rang. It was Warren.

"Hey, you!" he said when I answered. "What's up?"

"Nothing much," I said dryly as I visualized what I would wear during my Grammy performance.

"I know I was supposed to call you back so we could hook up, but I had a couple of client emergencies to tend to out of town. I just got in. Anything happening on your end?"

"Nothing much," I repeated, allowing my big news to bubble until I felt like letting it out of the pot.

"You sound salty," Warren said. "You mad at a brother or something?"

"Nope, just got a lot on my mind," I baited.

"Like what?" he bit.

"Well," I sighed, "I'm about to finalize my record deal, so things have been a little hectic. I'm making plans, considering moving to L.A., trying to decide—"

"Damn, girl! That's excellent!" Warren interrupted frantically. "We have to go out and celebrate. I'd been trying to get in touch with my boys over at One Time, but my schedule hasn't allowed me to do anything but work. I was trying to see when would be a good time for me to play your demo for them."

"Speaking of which," I said, "how did you like it?" Why had I just asked that? It really didn't matter anymore, did it? I was through with Warren, wasn't I?

Obviously I wasn't. There was no future in my fronting. I was still feeling Warren. I still wanted to be down with him. Down with the team. Down with the business pleasure partnership.

"How did I like the demo? Ahh, man." Warren sighed. "I haven't even had a chance to listen to it yet. In and out, in and out, that's how crazy it's been. You'll know how that is once you get your deal. But I'm on it. I'm going to check the tape out as soon as I get home. What's up with us hooking up? Tomorrow maybe?"

Say no. Say no. Say no. "That's cool" came out instead.

What the hell was I doing? Chance after chance, dis after dis. What was wrong with me?

"Good," Warren said. I could hear him cheesing through the phone. "Give me your address and I'll come scoop you at about eight."

As I rattled off my address, I kicked myself in the ass. Then I rubbed my sore butt and forgave myself. Maybe Warren really had been busy. After all, he was a manager with clients living everywhere. He had to tend to their needs. Now maybe he'd have time to tend to mine.

The next day I started preparing for my date early. This night would require the works. I was a soon-to-be singing sensation. My soon-to-be husband/business partner was here to stay. I walked into the bathroom and began getting ready. Long shower, shampooed hair, an eyebrow pluck, a facial, an extensive shave, a douche, a manicure, and a pedicure.

I walked into the bedroom to select something impeccable to wear. Mission accomplished. Red, clingy, silk jersey turtleneck. Red, low-waisted, hip-hugging cashmere pants. Red, draping, floor-length cashmere overcoat. Red leather boots with spiked silver heels. Thin silver chain belt to accentuate the waistline.

As I massaged scented lotion into my skin, the phone rang. It was the artist and repertoire executive at One Time Records. He told me that they had changed their minds. They had decided to sign a woman who was much younger than me and thinner than me, who wrote and produced her own music, made her own clothes, and directed her own music videos. He apologized, wished me well, said good-bye, and hung up quickly.

The bottle of lotion slipped out of my hand. Winds

below zero rushed through my bedroom. My lungs froze over. My eyes dried out. My lips cracked. My tongue stuck to the roof of my mouth. I sat motionless. I had no future. I would be stuck within the lowest ranks of corporate hell forever. I was officially cursed. I wanted to cry, but my tear ducts were frozen. Plus, tears would ruin my mascara.

I dummied up and managed to get dressed. I did still have Warren, didn't I? He would make me feel better, wouldn't he? He knew big people in bigger places. He would hook me up with another record company. Fuck One Time. They were just one of many. I forced myself to feel more confident. I was beautiful. I had a lovely voice. I was smart. I was talented enough to make it as a singer. Tonight, with my potential husband/partner by my side, would be just the beginning. I would look back on all this during my Grammy acceptance speech and laugh.

My doorbell rang at exactly eight o'clock. I took one last look in the mirror and opened the door. Warren's sweeping smile and roaming eye of approval eased my disappointment and anguish. The conversation in the car was lightweight and funny. I didn't tell him about One Time's phone call. We went to a sushi bar for dinner. The discussion got raw and sexy. I still didn't tell him about One Time's phone call. We went to a martini bar for dessert. The conversation got sweet and tangy. A high descended upon us. Now was the time to tell him about One Time's phone call.

"Let's make a toast," Warren slurred. "To your record deal, to me negotiating your lucrative contract, and to many, *many* album sales! To One Time!"

Tears gushed from my drunken red eyes as I watched watermelon-martini juice dribble down Warren's wobbly hand. I wanted to snatch his raised glass and throw it across the room. There would be no One Time record deal. There would be no lucrative contract. Warren would have to help me start all over from scratch. Pursue other record companies. Build another foundation and make a name for myself elsewhere. After our great date, I knew he'd be up to it.

"Why are you crying?" Warren asked, lowering his glass and grabbing my hand.

"Because . . . because . . . *there is no record deeeaaal*," I wailed. The whole bar turned and watched me throw my head into my hands and shake violently.

"Hey, hey, come on," Warren said. He wrapped his arm around my waist and led me outside. I bawled and slobbered all over his crisp white shirt. It was streaked with black mascara and soggy by the time we reached the car. He drove me home in silence as I sat half asleep and fully depressed.

"We can fix this, can't we?" I murmured.

"I'm sure you'll get picked up by somebody else," Warren replied.

"Will you make some calls for me? Will you put this back together?" I begged.

"I'll see what I can do, but I'm leaving town in the morning."

"What did you think of my demo?"

"I'm sure it's straight. I'll give it a listen when I get back."

We pulled up in front of my building. Warren reached over and opened my door from the inside of the car. He obviously had no intention of getting out and walking me to the door. Maybe he was too drunk. But so was I.

"Will you call me when you get back in town?" I asked, swinging one leg out of the car.

"We'll see."

"Can we sit down and discuss our strategy for sending out my demo tape?" I continued, swinging my other leg out of the car.

"Yeah," Warren responded dryly. Obviously his high was coming down. "I'm not sure when I'll be back, though."

"Okay. Maybe you can listen to my tape and call me while you're gone. It would at least be a start."

"We'll see," Warren repeated, shifting the car into drive and looking straight ahead. "Take care, okay?"

"Yeah," I spat, finally catching his hint to exit the vehicle immediately. "I guess this means you won't be coming upstairs."

"Early flight," he mumbled through a tight, artificially sweetened smile.

"Have a good trip," I choked inaudibly, getting out of the car and stumbling toward my building.

"Thanks," he said before pulling away, not even waiting for me to get inside.

Warren and I never talked again after that. When my glamorous record deal evaporated, so did he. I called and left him a couple of messages requesting my demo tape back, but he never returned it or my calls. Maybe he still thought I'd one day blow up and he wanted to have a piece of me on hand to prove that he knew me. But he obviously wanted no part of an up-and-comer for business *or* for pleasure. I hope someone told him I discontinued my pursuit of a singing career. My new underground project consists of me recruiting several friends and associates to work for my traveling massage/escort service and participate in my weekly mud-wrestling tournaments. I'm still trying to get that off the ground. Wish me luck.

> **Bottom Damn Line: Fuck a partnership. It's usually usury at its finest.**

Bubba the Bogus-Ass Baller

Have you ever thought you'd hit the jackpot? I have. His name was Bubba, and he was swimming in money. Bubba was a walking bank, and I wanted to open up an account. I wanted a key to the vault. I wanted to dig for gold. I wanted to plan an extremely early retirement and be a rich man's wife. I wanted to turn my debts and consolidations and responsibilities over to somebody else. I wanted to get paid just for lying in the shade. Bottom line, I wanted to ball.

I met Bubba one evening at a nightclub he owned. When I walked through the door, I immediately caught sight of him sitting in a VIP booth. This tycoon was dressed to the nines. Gucci down to the socks, rings and watch *filled* with rocks. Unlike Doug the Heinous Dragon, Bubba really was tall and attractive and husky like a football player. Flawless milk-chocolate skin, perfectly manicured nails, tailor-made pin-striped suit, shiny alligator shoes, jewels blinging in every direction, surrounded by plenty of other very important looking people, puffing on a cigar, and sipping cognac.

As my girlfriend and I walked past his table, I glanced over at Bubba and caught his eye. Our gaze lingered a little longer than necessary. I gave him a very slight, glossy smile before turning back around and following my friend to the other side of the club.

"Okay, okay, he looked at me!" I said, frantically waving my hands in the air.

"*Who* looked at you?" my girlfriend asked quizzically as we sat down at one of the peon tables.

"That chocolate delight sitting up front with all those other big players," I insisted, wondering how the derelict had missed him.

"*Him?*" she pointed, her face all scrunched up. "Girl, *please*. Why you always gotta go after the richest man in the room? You remember that time you stepped to Boris Kodjoe and got dissed?"

"Fuck him," I replied venomously. "I ain't like his punk ass no way!" (That was the bitterness coming out.) "And there's nothing wrong with shooting for the stars. But *anyway*, damn all that. Will you please help me devise a plan so that I can meet big daddy?"

"Yeah," my girlfriend laughed. "Lose about ten pounds, get some fake titties, a weave, and put on a G-string bikini!"

"You are such a bitch," I spat as I swiveled around in my seat and looked back over toward the VIP booth. All the big players were getting up to leave, and my chocolate dream was shaking their hands.

"They're leaving, they're leaving!" I declared, grabbing my friend's shoulder. "Should we go over there?"

"Well, he's by himself now," my friend said, getting up. "Come on, let's go over and see what he's talking about."

"No, I'm scared!" I shrieked, yanking on my friend's arm.

"Ah naw, don't be *scerred*," she smirked. "You shoot for the stars, remember?"

"Gimme some girl power first," I whined.

"Okay, girl power. You look good as hell and you don't seem to mind rejection, so take your ass over there and see what happens!"

"I hate you," I said, pulling myself together and walking toward his table.

As I approached my chocolate dream, he turned toward me and said, "Hey, I was going to ask if you and your girl wanted to join me earlier, but you walked off so fast I didn't get a chance. I figured you must have been looking for your man or something."

There is a God, I thought to myself as this cupcake smiled at me. "Oh, no, my friend was supposed to be meeting some people here," I lied so that he wouldn't know I was too much of a punk to stop before. "So we were looking for them."

"Did you find them?" he asked.

"Nope."

"Well, why don't you ladies join me? I'll have Kitty bring over some drinks."

"Thank you," I said, already sliding my frantic ass into the booth.

"You're welcome. By the way, I'm Bubba." After my friend and I introduced ourselves, Bubba walked over to the bar and took another cigar out of the display case. When he started talking to a woman who I assumed was Kitty the barmaid, I turned toward my girl with a Cheshire cat grin spread across my face.

"Gimme my props," I said.

"All praises due to you, 'cuz I'mo be drinking for free all night!" she exclaimed.

"You know what I mean!"

"Okay, you did it. You got Big Papa's attention. When you get his *number*, we'll talk."

"Whatever," I snapped, knowing I was already in there.

When Bubba got back to the table, he asked Kitty to bring over a bottle of Dom Pérignon. My friend pinched the skin off my forearm. Bubba greeted some of his guests, then turned to us and asked what we did for a living. After we both exaggerated drastically, Bubba lit his cigar and told us about his professional football-playing days, which had ended when a knee injury forced him into early retirement. As he sipped his cognac, he told us about how he'd begun investing in stocks and buying commercial and residential property. Smooth ass Bubba had it going on. In a very big way.

We continued to talk and continued to drink and, as the buzz ensued, began to laugh wildly. People stared longingly over at our table. At one point some woman walked up and said she'd wanted to stop by all night but was afraid to break up our assemblage. Then she zoomed in on me, held out a business card, and asked if I modeled. My friend, who was the tipsiest of us all, busted out laughing. I kicked the shit out of her underneath the table and she shut right up. Bubba looked over at me admiringly. I smiled my beauty-pageant smile, humbly said no, and took her card. The woman told me to call her, winked at me, then said good-bye and walked off.

"Looks like you've got an admirer," Bubba laughed.

"I don't swing that way," I responded.

"You two wanna go to another party with me?" Bubba asked.

"Sure," I said before my friend could even open her ine-briated mouth. She wasn't *about* to fuck up my marriage plans.

"Cool," Bubba replied, sliding out of the booth and tak-ing my hand to help me up. All eyes were on us as we walked out. The valet had Bubba's black S600 Mercedes parked right out front. We stepped in and drove all of one block to another club (you know ballers don't walk). Bubba parked the car right out front, and we followed him straight past the ton of people standing in line outside the door. He greeted everyone, had his name checked off on the guest list, and led us straight inside to the VIP room.

When we got past the velvet rope, the owner of the club walked up and hugged Bubba. Rappers and singers lined the bar. Actors and actresses cluttered the dance floor. NBA and NFL players were scattered everywhere in between. My groupie ass was in seventh heaven.

Bubba introduced us to the club's owner, who invited us over to his table. My friend was stunned speechless by the whole scene, but I, on the other hand, fronted like I was unfazed and strutted coolly by Bubba's side. The owner's table was filled with beautiful people. We introduced our-selves, and I sat down and watched as my girl gave the owner the big eye. *Good*, I thought to myself. *Now that she's off my back I can climb all over Bubba's.*

Some supermodel ordered another round of Cristal. An MC finally succumbed to the DJ's pressure and started freestyling on the mic. The owner of the club was now all up in my girl's grill. Bubba started whispering sweet nothings in my ear. Someone was keeping my glass filled to the rim. Pounds of lobster and shrimp were delivered to our table. I was reminded of why I'd been put here on this earth. I was born to ball.

After hours of unbelievable fun and excitement, we left the club. Bubba dropped us off at my car. He handed me a business card. I handed him my home, work, cell, and pager numbers. He promised we would get together again soon. I told him I'd love that. He gave me an expensive cigar to give to my boss in order to win points at work. I held him close and kissed him amorously on the cheek, thanking God that He'd finally revealed my soul mate. Long gone were my mere thoughts of Bubba's money, status, and notoriety. I was now in love with the man, the myth, the *legend*.

I looked at Bubba's business card the next morning and realized that it listed only his club's general phone number. No personal numbers. Not even a private business line. *A simple oversight* is what I called it as I rushed to a gift shop. I had to buy Bubba a thank-you card in order to show my appreciation for the wonderful evening we'd shared. My true purpose in sending the card was to offer Bubba an added incentive to call me.

I combed each and every aisle of the store in search of the most exquisite, artistic blank card available. It took me over an hour to find it. When I did, I flipped it over and saw the eight-dollar price tag. Tax not included. I didn't care.

I pulled up in front of the nearest mailbox and penned the most eloquent, sincere thank-you note I could muster up. I wanted my future husband to know exactly how much I appreciated his graciousness and generosity. Through this card, I wanted to subliminally tell him that I'd be a considerate wife and wouldn't take him or his money for granted. I would take good care of our children and personal affairs so that he could concentrate on his business. I would remain at the top of my game by working out and getting my hair, nails, and feet done on a regular basis. I would get facials, massages, and even a Brazilian wax if he liked that sort of thing. I would dress to kill each and every day. I would hire the best help to cook and clean. I would satisfy him, stay out of his way, not spend *too* much of his money, and love him like he deserved to be loved. I had lost my goddamn mind, knew it at the time, and didn't care. I signed my name, dropped the card in the mail, and waited.

Bubba called two days later and thanked me for the card. He told me that no one ever thanked him for the things he did and that he appreciated my acknowledgment. I told him I wouldn't be able to sleep nights if I were an ungrateful person. He told me he wanted to see me again. I asked him when. He said he'd call back and let me know. I said okay. He never did.

Bubba had slipped through my fingers like air. It was time for Plan B. I wasn't ready to give up just yet. I tried calling him at the club several times, but he was never available. I began getting desperate. I made my girl come over and tell me what the hell I should do next. She came up with an ingenious idea. She suggested that we go back up to his club. I kissed her dead on the lips with gratitude. She almost slapped the shit out of me.

The next night we visited Bubba's club again. I was decked out in a fitted, deep purple, Japanese-style jacket, a miniskirt with a slit up to here, fishnet stockings, and knee-high boots. I was the cat's meow. All eyes were on me as I walked through the door. But I didn't want any of those busters. I had to remain faithful to my soul mate, Bubba.

We looked around and realized that he wasn't there. So we sat down, ordered drinks, and waited. And waited. And waited. At two-thirty in the morning my friend gave up and said we needed to go home. It was damn near time for us to go to work. My heart decomposed.

I called my girl the next day at work. Time for Plan C. She was helpful and patient with me because I'd supported her stupidity in the past. She checked Bubba's Web site and suggested that we go back to the club later on that week for a comedy show. Another ingenious idea. I kissed her through the phone.

It was raining heavily the night of the show. We didn't get to the club until after eleven o'clock. We were late as hell. When I tried to open the door, it was locked. I was about to cry when my friend rolled her eyes and banged on it. To my surprise, the club's manager opened it. He looked at us like we were crazy. I asked what time the show had started. He said seven o'clock and indicated that the club was now closed. I batted my eyelashes and asked if Bubba was there. He said he didn't know, asked for my name, then said he'd go check. He closed the door and locked it, leaving us outside to wait in the downpour.

My friend stood there, totally appalled. I stood there in horrific anticipation. My insides rumbled and my crotch prickled. I knew damn well that Bubba was there and that the manager had just gone to find out whether or not he wanted to be bothered with me. I felt like O.J. the moment before the verdict was read. My gut told me I was headed for the electric chair. As I grabbed my friend's hand for moral support, the manager opened the door and let us in. I felt like O.J. the moment after the verdict was read.

Bubba was sitting in the same booth we had all partied in the night we'd met. The sight felt painfully nostalgic. Bubba got up, hugged us, and immediately apologized to me for not calling. As I looked into his eyes and noticed the redness and bags, Bubba slumped down into his seat and talked about how exhausted he was. He swore it wasn't about another woman (as if I'd had a right to ask). He had been laying a new floor in another nightclub he'd just bought, he had family from out of town staying with him, his assistant manager had just quit, and he was having trouble finding a new company to manage the majority of his property.

I felt so stupid and small and unimportant and insignificant. I wanted some business, too. I wanted to tell Bubba that I could be of so much assistance to him. I wanted him to know that I cared, that I could get him through these difficult times, that he needed me in his life. I figured that now, since he'd let us into the club after hours when he was thoroughly exhausted, I at least had a foot in the door. This was a new beginning. Things would start rolling from this point forward.

During our conversation, the club's chef brought a huge plate of chicken fingers and french fries over to the table. Bubba told us to help ourselves and had the manager fix us drinks. The three of us sat there talking, laughing, joking, and eating off that one plate. It was camaraderie at its finest. Close, intimate, unguarded, and personal. The struggle was over. The chase had ended. My head was above water. Bubba had finally let me in. I left the club with a renewed spirit.

Three weeks passed. No word from Bubba. I'd broke down on a few occasions and called him, but as always, he was never available. Bubba hadn't given me a personal number the night of the chicken fingers, but at that point I wasn't worried about it. I'd thought I was in there. What was his deal? What had gone wrong? Had there been some sort of chemical mix-up? Because I could have sworn our elements had converged. Obviously I'd misread the formula.

I was in a state of misery. I was straight vexed. I knew I couldn't call my friend for help in coming up with Plan D because she wouldn't be having it. This had gone too far. I knew I needed to move on, but my tires of progression were stuck in the mud.

So I sat and I thought. And I thought. And I thought. And finally I came up with an idea that was brighter than all the rest. Bubba's birthday was coming up, so I decided to send him a gift. I'd buy him something precious and rare. I'd buy him something so fabulous and clever that he would have no choice *but* to get with me. His heart would force him to. Whoever he opened it in front of would force him to. Whoever he told about it would force him to.

Now for the hard part. What would I buy? What do you get for a man who has everything? I couldn't go to his house in a trench coat, thong, and fuck-me pumps because I didn't know where he lived. I couldn't send him something outrageously expensive because my rent was due. So I sat and I thought. And I thought. And I thought. And then, right before I decided to jump in the lake and end it all, my mind gave birth to the most extraordinary idea possible.

The night I'd met Bubba, we'd talked about elementary school and everything we missed about it. The main thing Bubba remembered was his strong craving for grape Hubba Bubba bubble gum. He remembered the day when his fourth-grade teacher, who he'd had a huge crush on, confiscated his brand-new pack of grape Hubba Bubba. After that, his love for her quickly turned to hate. He despised the teacher for the rest of the year for taking away his most beloved treat.

So, after remembering that cute little story, I decided to send Bubba some grape Hubba Bubba bubble gum for his birthday. It was thoughtful, meaningful, observant, creative, and kind. More importantly, I hoped that his strong craving for the bubble gum would induce a strong craving for me.

I searched high and low for that damn gum. I think I went to about ten stores before I finally found it. I bought the last six packs, then went home and searched through my Christmas closet for the packaging. I ended up finding a perfect small, flat, shiny gold box that had a beautiful black velvet bag inside. The packs of gum fit inside perfectly. I wrapped the bag in iridescent tissue paper and placed it gently inside the gold box. I wrapped the box in thick, dark metallic paper and tied it with a satiny cream ribbon. I signed the elegant birthday card I'd bought him and placed it at an angle underneath the ribbon.

The next day, I went to the mailroom at work and stole a "Happy Birthday" mailing package that was supposed to be for clients only. The package was black and shiny and fancy and decorated with colorful balloons and confetti. After sliding the gift and card inside, I neatly sealed it shut, typed out a mailing label, and stuck it onto the front. Then I called our messenger service and told them I had an emergency package that needed to be delivered immediately. I also told them that I wanted someone to call and let me know when the package was delivered, who delivered it, and who signed for it. I got a call forty-seven minutes after the package was picked up from my office with all of the requested information. Now all I could do was wait.

I was on edge all day. Bubba didn't call me at work, but I knew he probably wouldn't get to the club and find the gift until later on that night. I got home from work at about five-thirty and set up shop by the phone. Cookies, television remote, magazines, blanket, chips, and red Kool-Aid. I was set.

My phone rang at 8:34 P.M. It was my girlfriend. I told her I would call her back. My phone rang at 8:47 P.M. It was my other girlfriend. I told her I couldn't talk. My phone rang at 9:06 P.M. It was my mother. I told her no, Bubba hadn't called yet. My phone rang at 9:17 P.M. It was Leroy the Loser-Ass Liar, claiming he'd just joined the Harlem Globetrotters. I told him to kiss my ass and hung up in his face. My phone rang at 9:32 P.M. It was Bubba. My heart shot right out of my chest.

"Hey," he said.

"Hey!" I replied frantically, now up on my feet and pacing the floor. "Happy Birthday!"

"Thank you!" he shouted as music and voices blasted in the background.

"Are you at the club?" I asked nervously, already knowing the answer.

"Yeah, and I just opened your gift," Bubba responded. I could hear him smiling through the phone.

"Ask her, man, ask her," I heard several people saying in the background.

"Hey, let me ask you something," Bubba began. I was now sitting on the floor, rocking back and forth like Sybil. "Did I tell you that grape Hubba Bubba was my favorite thing back when I was in elementary school?"

"Yes, you did. The night that I met you," I spewed, warm goo oozing through my veins.

"I knew it! Man!" Bubba ranted. "I did tell her, and she remembered," he told the people in the background.

"That was dope as hell," I heard somebody say. "That was, dude," someone else chimed in. I was absolutely elated.

"Okay, you all get out of my office now so I can talk privately," Bubba told them.

As I waited for the people to leave, every hair on my body stood straight up. My time had finally come. For real. Perseverance is the key. And I had stayed in there. Now the chase was finally over. I had sweated my ass off and was dehydrated as hell, but I'd made it past the finish line. My award-winning plan couldn't have gone better. The result? Bubba loved my gift, Bubba's friends loved my gift, Bubba loved me, and Bubba's friends loved me, too. *It's all good now, I'm out the hood now*, I sang to myself as I wondered how many carats my ring would be.

"Hey," Bubba said softly, pulling me out of my daydream.

"I'm here," I murmured.

"I *love* your gift," he began, his gratitude slowly trickling through my ear and into my heart. "That was so sweet and thoughtful. I got a ton of gifts, too, and a lot of them were really expensive. But that doesn't matter. Yours takes the cake. I can't believe you remembered that story about the gum, and I *really* can't believe you thought to give it to me as a birthday gift." Bubba paused for a moment and took a breath. "I mean, I just . . . that was so thoughtful. The best gift I got. Thank you."

"Oh, you're welcome," I gushed, close to tears at that point. I couldn't believe he was so moved by what I'd done. I'd definitely wanted this reaction from him, but actually getting it felt amazing.

"Listen, I've got to go," Bubba said. "They need me upstairs."

"Okay," I said, my heart dropping down to my ass. I didn't want to get off the phone. I wanted to talk some more. I wanted to see him. I wanted him to want to see me. Now. I wanted him to invite me over to his crib, to the club, *wherever*. I just wanted be with him again. The fear of me hanging up that phone and never talking to or seeing him again hit, and the impact of the blow was excruciating.

"Can I take you to lunch?" Bubba asked. I heard pages flipping in the background. I assumed it was his calendar.

"Bubba, listen," I sighed. "I know you're really busy, and you haven't had any time to see me thus far. I'd just prefer it if you'd be honest, and if you don't think this is going to happen, then say that. I sent you the gift and you thanked me. Don't feel obligated to take me out—"

"*No*, no, it's not like that," Bubba interrupted ardently. "I know I haven't called, but I've been *so* tied up. Are you free Tuesday?"

"Yes," I said before I knew it.

"Okay, I have to be at the club early that morning, so we can do lunch that afternoon. I'm putting you down on my calendar as we speak."

For some reason, the whole calendar thing made me feel as if our plans were indestructible. "Are we going to have lunch at the club?" I asked, hoping he'd say yes. That way, if I came to where he would be, he'd have no other choice *but* to have lunch with me. If not, there would be a much bigger possibility that he'd stand me up.

"No, I'm going to pick you up and take you somewhere nice. I'll call you that morning to confirm, okay? They're calling me from upstairs again, so I need to get going. I'll see you Tuesday."

"Okay," I said before slowly hanging up the phone. I didn't know whether to be happy, sad, hopeful, or mournful. So for the time being, I decided not to be anything.

Tuesday came. My morning routine took two hours instead of my normal thirty minutes. I gave it everything I had, plus a whole lot more. Freshly shampooed and flat-ironed hair, extra makeup, big-money power suit, and conservatively sexy pumps. When I finally got to work, everybody asked if I had a job interview. My boss was extra nice to me. I got no work done whatsoever because I was too busy staring at the phone, eagerly anticipating its ring.

Tuesday went. Bubba didn't call. I never saw or heard from him again.

Bottom Damn Line: Fuck Bubba.

III

Unholy Matrimony

The trouble with some women is that they get all excited
about nothing—and then marry him.

—CHER

Unholy Matrimony

There are those of us who get lonely. Who get desperate. Who get bored, weak, retarded, and horny. We get so out of sorts that we forget how to function. We become irritable. Disagreeable. Impatient. Immoral. We wonder why. It is because we need a better half in our lives. By any means necessary.

So we search. And seek. And seek. And search. For a long time. And find no one. Which makes us feel frustrated. Hopeless. Destitute. Neglected. But not enough to take us all the way under. We are still here. So we must keep looking. It is the only way to survive. So we give it one last good ole college try.

We come up with an alternative plan. A less adequate plan. A plan that will tamper with our standards. Modify our ideals. Alter our ethics. Force us to settle for just a half. Not a better half. Just a half. And under the most extreme circumstances, we settle for even less than a half.

Halves and less than halves do not live up to the Plan A players. Plan A players are single, attractive, funny, and smart. Plan B players are not. Plan B players are usually ugly, personality-less, full of shit, and/or attached. But they're willing. Willing to get with our desperate asses. So we're able. Able to adjust to their defective asses. Suddenly, ugly is sufficient. Personality is unimportant. Bullshit is acceptable. As for girlfriends? They're invisible. As for fiancées? They're irrelevant. Deprivation does not allow us to think of others. Solitude has forced us to act now and pay later.

Then there are those of us who are mindless warriors. When we see something we want, we've got to have it. We will fight for it. We don't care who it belongs to. We are better than who it belongs to anyway. So we're going to get it. By any means necessary. But the means won't be extensive, considering that we think we can get anybody we want. We can't, and it's obvious, but we still believe we can.

People like us attempt to break the strongest unions. Destroy the happiest homes. Increase the divorce rate. We have no regard for marriage. We're too cute to worry about that. Our butts are too big to worry about that. Wedding bands are too thin to worry about that. And we know how to play the game in order to win the prize, too. Our promises of discretion warrant guiltless indulgence. Our bedside manner alleviates all vows of monogamy. Our skillful demeanor prevents us from being found out. Personal desires prevent us from considering others' feelings. From considering the consequences. We feel shafted, not guilty. We feel owed, not responsible. Bottom line: since all men and women were supposedly created equal, we feel that the blessed should share with the less fortunate.

Then there are those of us who do respect relationships. Who do regard commitments. Who do believe in till death do us part. We may be lonely, but we refuse to take it out on others. We may be jealous, but we refuse to let that break a bond. We may be craving, but we refuse to give in to wrongful lust. Promises are more important than empty passion. Emotions are more important than manipulative flattery. Vows are more important than brief encounters.

Those who are attached should step off. Those who are becoming unattached should finalize now and approach later. Those who are newly unattached and qualified to approach should be fully recovered from their previous predicaments. We are not in the mood to psychoanalyze. We just want a healthy relationship. We are not in the mood to hypothesize. So we expect straightforward behavior. We are not in the mood for issues. So we hope that they have all been resolved. We know we are probably asking for too much. So we're not surprised when things don't go as planned. When it comes to the engagements, marriages, and divorces of others, things usually never do.

Forrest the Foul Fiancé

Have you ever dated a whore? A prostitute who worked for free? I have. His name was Forrest, and he was the best lay I've ever had.

But the situation was wrong from the start. When I met Forrest, he had a woman. When I dismissed Forrest's advances, he still had a woman. When I finally got with Forrest, his woman had become his fiancée. When Forrest got married, I stuck around. It had been a long haul. I was the emperor of idiocy for what now seems like forever. But it's finally over. So I can proceed to dog his stank nasty, perverted, disgusting, offensive, unscrupulous ass out.

I met Forrest at a friend's house. It was love at first sight for him, irrefutable indifference for me. He didn't look like much, with his sallow complexion, beady eyes, unkempt hair, and *almost* designer outfit. Word on the street was that he wasn't about shit, had a good woman who he took for granted, and was always on the prowl for fresh new ass.

When we were introduced, I noticed him giving me the big eye, so I ran the other way. But Forrest was persistent. Forrest had excellent follow-up skills. Forrest was not going to leave me alone until I gave in to his whims.

So finally, after a relentless, sweat-filled, salivating chase for him and a vulnerable, lonely, desolate time for me, Forrest managed to crack my egg and drink my yolk. He started off smart and slow. He was sweet, attentive, and considerate as hell. He took me to nice restaurants, bought me expensive gifts, and showered me with attention. He let me chill at his magnificent house, swim in his marble Jacuzzi, and sleep in his big water bed whenever I wanted, without him ever laying a hand on me. He told me he'd leave his woman for me. He told me I was much prettier than she was. He told me he wasn't sure about settling down with her. He said he was infatuated with me. But I didn't believe him. I didn't want to commit to a promiscuous man like him anyway. He was just something to do. A mere basket of bread as I waited on my entrée.

Then one night, when Forrest and I were snuggling on his couch watching television, he kissed me. I was caught totally off guard. I just sat there with my immobile mouth slightly open. Forrest gently caressed my lips with his, then stroked my lips with his tongue and glided his fingertips along the back of my neck. I glanced to the left, then glanced to the right in utter confusion. I'd known something like this was going to happen eventually, but not tonight. I wasn't mentally prepared tonight. But Forrest didn't care. Forrest was persistent.

I couldn't deny it. The kisses felt good. So I kissed him back. And before I knew it, my willpower slipped out of my mouth right along with my tongue. I was gone. That was the best damn kissing I'd ever taken part in. Firmly soft, swiftly slow, passionate, erotic, fiery, and lustful. My face in his hands, our tongues dancing a jig, his lips sucking mine, my teeth teasing his earlobe, his teeth tickling my neck. It was the kind of foreplay that preceded a five-star show.

Forrest suggested that we go upstairs to his bedroom. I silently obliged. He laid me down gently on his bed and slowly removed my clothes. I didn't care that my bra was black velvet and my panties were pink satin. Forrest didn't seem to care either. As I lay there totally nude, he stood over me and smiled triumphantly. Then he removed his clothes and joined me. His skin felt so warm and silky against mine. My breasts felt so good inside his mouth. His genitalia felt overwhelmingly big and hard against my thigh. I was getting more and more excited by the second. Something was dribbling down my leg. I realized that it was coming from me. Forrest ran his tongue along the lining of my belly button and moved down toward the end of the bed. Then his head disappeared between my legs.

Forrest had the tongue of a wizard. His technique was majestic. His skill was superior. I instantly regretted making him chase me for so long. Look at what I'd been missing! I felt my control slipping away. Ecstasy began to take over. Forrest had me beating the bed like a captured brute. Squealing like a wounded boar. I was drenched in sweat. My body went into cardiac arrest. I died and went to heaven. When I came back to life, a blurry-looking Forrest was grinning in my face, asking if I was okay. I just lay there, comatose, waiting for my eyes to stop dilating. Forrest didn't care that he'd just murdered me. He was too busy rolling on a condom. I wanted to plead for a recovery period. But I couldn't utter a single word.

When Forrest inserted his magic wand, my eyes rolled into the back of my head and my eyelids fluttered furiously. I started ripping at the sheets. My body began to jerk up and down, back and forth. My head did a 360-degree turn. I spewed pea soup. It looked like a scene straight from *The Exorcist*.

Forrest flipped me over onto my stomach. I was a surfboard, riding the waves of paradise. After the tide passed, Forrest threw me up on top of him. I was Elizabeth Taylor in *National Velvet*. I conquered all the hurdles and puddles and won the blue ribbon.

Then Forrest gently laid me on my back, wrapped my legs around his waist, and lightly kissed every inch of my face. He sprinkled my shoulders with tender strokes of his tongue. He floated in and out and around and around with a soft, slow, fluid motion. He nuzzled my neck with his lips and breathed fragrant words in my ear. He wrapped his arms around me securely and stared lovingly into my eyes. He told me that he wanted to feel this way forever. He told me that he wanted to be mine. He told me that I was his. Then he climaxed. Then I climaxed. Then I came back down to earth.

Forrest and I continued our affair but kept it on the hush. Only his closest friends and my closest friends knew about it. He had all of his friends wanting to sleep with me. I had all of my friends wanting to sleep with him. It was an ill situation. And it only got iller. Eventually, Forrest stopped asking me to be his. We stopped going out on legitimate dates. He moved out of his house and in with his girlfriend. I could no longer swim in his Jacuzzi and lie on his water bed. The affair became tight and harder to maintain, which made it all the more exciting. *Whenever, wherever, whatever* became our motto. We were out of control. We were addicted to each other. And while he managed to keep both his girlfriend and me in his life, I managed to ignore the fact that we were going absolutely nowhere. Fast.

One day, I realized that I hadn't heard from Forrest in a while. I'd call him, but he wouldn't call me back. He wouldn't return my pages. I was in a state of confusion. I caught up with one of his friends one night at a poetry reading. I pulled him aside and asked where the hell Forrest had been. "Did he move?" I asked. "Is he all right?" His friend just stood there with a pitiful look on his face. I followed him outside as he proceeded to tell me that Forrest had taken his girlfriend on an exotic vacation and proposed to her.

My tolerance went bankrupt. My senses shut down. My saliva turned to grit. I threw my coat, my purse, and my notebook down on the ground and went the fuck off. Forrest's friend backed away from me in fear. I stood in the middle of the street and carried on like a madwoman. I couldn't believe that Forrest hadn't told me. I couldn't believe that he'd just left me out here to find out from whoever. He'd just dropped me like I'd never existed. He'd just played me so very greasy and so very cheap.

My friends walked over, picked up everything I'd dropped, put my coat on me backward so that it fit like a straitjacket, and carried me off to the car. I screamed and hollered the whole way there. I screamed and hollered the whole way home. I paged Forrest the minute I walked through the door and left him a voice-mail message so vile, so irate, that he had no choice but to call back and explain himself.

Forrest apologized immediately. He almost cried. But almost didn't count. He told me that he'd been backed into a corner and that marriage was the only way out. I told him that still didn't excuse the fact that I'd had to hear about it from someone else. He said he hadn't known how to tell me because he didn't want to hurt my feelings. I told him I wasn't buying that. He told me to meet him over at his boy's house so that he could apologize in person. I told him I was on my way.

I begged myself not to be hurt. I'd always known he had a girlfriend and I'd always known he'd eventually marry her. I'd known she wasn't having it any other way. I didn't want Forrest for myself anyway. She could have his lying, cheating punk ass. I was glad I wasn't the one stuck with him. I wanted to be with a real man. I didn't want to settle. But I was still in my car on my way to see him. And I couldn't come up with a good explanation as to why. So I settled on the fact that I was bored and needed something to do. I was nothing but an idle mind, building monuments of trouble in the devil's workshop.

Then one day my period didn't come. But I wasn't pregnant. I was just stressed out. I wasn't on the Pill anymore, but Forrest had told me he'd pulled out extra early the last time we were together. I wasn't going to worry about it. I would just hold off and wait because I knew my period was on its way. No big deal. My friends said that I wasn't pregnant, too. They reminded me that I was under a lot of pressure at work. They reminded me that I'd been exercising constantly. We all knew that my body was just going through some changes.

A month passed and my body was still going through some changes, plus a whole lot more. I'd been feeling nauseated and started hating my favorite foods. Everything smelled ten times stronger. I was sick to my stomach late at night and early in the morning. Dizzy spells attacked at any given moment. My stomach was flipping around in ways that it had never flipped before. One of my friends forced me to take a pregnancy test. The results were positive. I was devastated.

I told myself this wasn't happening to me. I was too old for this shit. I wasn't supposed to get pregnant until I was happily married and ready for a baby. I called my doctor's office and got the number for an abortion clinic. I called and asked when I could come in. They told me four weeks after my missed period. I scheduled an appointment, as the thought of carrying the burden any longer nauseated me even further.

I tried calling Forrest but couldn't get in touch with him. He wasn't returning my pages. I finally broke down and called one of his friends. He told me that Forrest was on his honeymoon. I didn't even know he'd gotten married. I willed myself not to cry, then called my girlfriend and asked her to go to the clinic with me. She said of course.

Eventually, Forrest called me at work. I wasted no time in telling him what was going on. He was even more devastated than I was. He gasped like a bitch about to have an asthma attack. He asked what I was going to do. Not *we*, just *I*.

"What do you think I'm going to do?" I snapped. I wanted to say a whole lot more but decided against it. How could I complain? I'd known who I was involved with long before this happened. It was *I* who had chosen to continue participating.

"Oh, thank *God*," Forrest sighed.

"What?" I spat.

"I'm sorry," Forrest added quickly. "It's just that . . . a lot has been going on lately."

"Yeah, like you funning in the sun with your new wife while I'm here going through this mess alone," I snapped. "You don't know about a lot going on."

"You're not the only one I got pregnant," Forrest blurted out.

"Your wife is pregnant too?" I asked, totally stunned.

"No." Forrest paused, shuffled the phone around, then cleared his throat. "This other woman who I'd been seeing."

That round of ammunition shot through the phone so forcefully that it shattered my entire being. "Who is she?" I choked as I stabbed a sharp metal envelope opener deep into my wooden desktop over and over again.

"Nobody, just a woman I'd met. We were dating before I got engaged, and I never told her I had a girlfriend. Then she found out that I had gotten engaged and stopped speaking to me."

"Then she found out she was pregnant?" I asked, hoping I could get in to take an HIV test that weekend.

"No. We, uhh, we eventually started talking again. And she got pregnant after that. She had the baby three weeks before my wedding."

Highly explosive devices started going off in my uterus. I prayed to God that He'd deliver me from this purgatory.

After about ten minutes of complete silence, I finally asked, "Does your wife know?"

"Yeah," he replied shamefully.

"Did she know before she *married* you?" I asked.

"Yeah," he replied shamefully.

"And she still *married* you?" I asked.

"Yeah," he replied shamefully.

I swallowed over and over and over again so that I wouldn't vomit all over my desk.

"When are you going?" he asked.

"This weekend," I managed.

"*Damn*, I'll be out of town," he said.

"Figures," I huffed, my head now embedded in my hand.

"Do you have anyone who can take you?" he asked.

"Of course," I responded.

"Are you mad at me?" he asked.

"Does it matter? At this point I just want to get through this and be okay," I said.

"You will, you will," he replied, his voice lowering several octaves, as if he was ready to get off the phone.

"Uh, before you go, can we discuss the financial arrangements?" I asked.

"Well, my money's kinda tight right now because I had to pay for the wedding," he stammered, as convincingly as possible. "Do you think you could come up with some of the money, too?"

"You know what?" I began, now squeezing my rubber stress ball to the point of possible combustion. "I can't discuss this with you any further because I don't want to get fired. I'll be at your job tomorrow to pick up the money. Now is the *wrong* time to fuck with me, so don't."

I hung up in his face, went to the bathroom, made sure no one else was there, locked myself in the very last stall, and cried my eyes out.

When I got to Forrest's job the next day, I called upstairs and told him to come down. When he did, I was sitting in my car and holding my hand out the window, not wanting any conversation whatsoever.

"Hey! You look good," he gushed, cheesing all over the goddamn place like this was a conjugal visit or something.

"Thank you," I responded drily, my hand still out.

"You coming up?" he asked, taking my outstretched hand in his and rubbing it against his crotch. "At least we won't have to worry about protection."

I snatched my hand out of his and punched the shit out of his balls. He fell to the ground and rolled around in agony. I got out of the car, flipped his ass over onto his back, dug deep into his pockets, and confiscated every last goddamn cent. Then I grabbed hold of his collar and yanked him up so that his face was millimeters away from mine.

"I *told* you not to fuck with me," I spat. Then I threw his ass back down, jumped into my car, and sped off. When I got onto the expressway, I realized that only half of the money was there. I called Forrest and told him that if he didn't have his ass outside of my job the very next day at twelve o'clock with the rest of the money, I would call his wife, tell her everything, *and* have his baby.

The very next day Forrest was outside waiting at eleven-thirty sharp. I walked through the revolving door of my building into warm, sunny weather. The contradiction between it and the storm occurring throughout my insides was overwhelming. The mere sight of Forrest was disgusting. I walked up to him and didn't utter one word. I just took the money that was in his hand, turned around, and walked away.

"I'll call you while I'm out of town to make sure everything goes okay," Forrest said to my back. I just waved him off and kept on going.

When I got back to my desk, I realized that all the money *still* wasn't there. I immediately grabbed the phone and started dialing Forrest's home number to see if his wife was there. But then I stopped and thought about it. Why put her through any more hell? Her trick-ass husband and bastard stepchild were bad enough. I hung the phone up and focused solely on getting myself through this.

Saturday came. It was traumatic and painful. My girl who took me was understanding and supportive. I recovered at her apartment. I felt fragile and vulnerable. But I was okay. And I would get better. And I would forge ahead. And I would never be that stupid again. Forrest never called to check on me, the way he'd promised he would.

It took him a whole week to finally call. I was so through I wouldn't even talk to him. He had to call my friend and ask how I was doing. She wanted to tell him that I'd changed my mind and decided to have the baby out of spite, but instead decided to just tell him the truth.

As I moved on and got away from Forrest, his baby's mama did the total opposite. She had him take a blood test.

She took him to court for child support. She and her friends put the word out on the street about their illegitimate baby. She gave the baby Forrest's last name. All of his friends and associates found out about it. Some of them even saw the baby and told Forrest it looked just like him. The gossip humiliated and devastated his wife. The couple eventually fled the country—wifey out of embarrassment, Forrest out of guilt. I was thrilled to have him that much farther away from me. We never spoke again.

Bottom Damn Line: Fuck settling for something to do. See where it gets you?

Marvin the Married Man-Boy

I hate married men. Married men are so fucking stupid. Married men are such fucking punks. And married men are so fucking irresistible. Why? Because their wives have gone to work to make them that way. Wives clean husbands up and pull them together. Take them from ashy to classy. Create a good, clean, polished look for them. Dress them well. Give them good senses of humor and good personalities. Co-sign on their nice cars. Put big houses and husbands' businesses in their names. Act as the masterminds behind their husbands' businesses. Decorate the beautiful houses that their husbands invite their mistresses to during lunch breaks and on weekends when their wives are out of town visiting relatives. Bottom line: next to every good man is an even gooder woman who made him that way and who he still manages to cheat on and treat like shit.

Which leads me to my story about Marvin. Marvin was a Greek god. He was six foot three with perfectly chiseled features and a perfectly chiseled body. He looked like an Olympic gold medalist. He acted like the funny, caring, smart, affectionate type of man who I could come home to every night. I would never tire of his looks. I would never tire of his charisma. He'd make me feel loved. He'd make me feel desirable. He'd make me feel as if I counted. As if I mattered. As if he weren't married. But he was. So I couldn't win. I tried. But I couldn't.

Marvin's wife had made him into the man he was when we met. She was the one who'd grown up on the prestigious side of town, but during high school she had still managed to take on Marvin, who'd grown up in the ghetto, as her charity case. She was the one who became his sweetheart and encouraged him to play his heart out on the basketball court so that he could earn a full scholarship to college. When he did, she was the one who followed him there and encouraged him to shoot for the NBA as well as earn a degree in business administration. When he graduated and didn't make it to the NBA, she was the one who encouraged him to attend graduate school with her and earn an MBA. When they graduated, she was the one who encouraged him to marry her. When he did, she was the one who encouraged him to open up a chain of southern-style restaurants. When he did, I was the one who walked into one of them and immediately fell in love with him.

The restaurant wasn't technically open the first time I went there. It was during the holiday season, I was driving past on the way to my mother's house, and I was starving. The lights were on, so I pulled over. The door was unlocked, so I walked in.

The restaurant was nice and homey, with warm lighting, cozy booths, and country-motif hangings on the walls. No customers were there, but I didn't care. I just needed to get my eat on right quick. Marvin the Greek god came out of what I assumed was the kitchen. Our eyes locked. My heart stopped. My jaw dropped. I wished I'd put on some makeup before leaving home. But he still looked impressed. So I felt blessed. Then I felt sinful, because I wanted him to throw me on top of the counter and have his way with me. But he couldn't. Because we weren't alone. Some little short, fat, cheerful-looking woman with a played-out feathered haircut, wearing navy blue stretch pants and an oversized gray sweatshirt, had just walked out of what I assumed was the kitchen. I wanted the cook to go away so that the Greek god and I could get our conversation on. But this was no cook. This was the Greek god's wife.

"Hi." She smiled bubbly at me. Then she turned toward the Greek god and said, "Honey, where did Miguel put the pancake batter?"

"In the big fridge in the back," the Greek god replied, his eyes still on me.

"Oh, good," she exclaimed, clapping her hands. Then she turned to me and said, "I'm Dolly."

How appropriate, I thought as I smiled back and introduced myself.

Dolly must have missed the lust in my face and the drool hanging from her husband's chin, because all she said was "Nice meeting you," before turning around and walking back into what I assumed was the kitchen. I love a woman who knows her place.

"It certainly is nice meeting you," the Greek god murmured, riding off his wife's statement. "I'm Marvin." He held out his hand and shook mine for entirely too long.

"Are you open?" I asked.

"For you I am," he replied.

"So this must be your spot," I guessed.

"It is," he confirmed.

"Well, I'm starving. But if you're not really open, I guess no one's cooking."

"My wife is making me some pancakes right now. Why don't I tell her to put some on for you, too?" Marvin asked, already walking toward what I assumed was the kitchen.

I felt uncomfortable. I didn't want this man's wife cooking for me. They weren't even open. She'd question his bending of the rules. She'd tell him she wasn't about to make shit for no bitch. She'd come out of the kitchen with a butcher knife and try to kill me. But instead, several minutes later, she came out of what I now knew was the kitchen with a stack of pancakes and turkey bacon in one hand, her coat in the other, and Marvin behind her.

"Enjoy, you guys. I'm running home to start dinner. Take care." She smiled at me. "I hope you come back and see us again." Then she walked out the door.

Damn, I thought to myself. Now I couldn't fuck her husband because she was too damn nice. Or maybe I *could* fuck her husband because she was so damn stupid. I wish I *would* leave my husband alone with a dime piece such as myself. It's an accidental affair just waiting to happen.

"Have a seat," Marvin said after he grabbed a little glass pitcher of syrup from behind the counter and sat down at a booth. I sat down across from him. He grinned. I grinned. We were like two schoolchildren, cutting class and eating breakfast during lunchtime.

"Thank you," I replied, taking a plate and utensils from the other side of the table. "I want three pancakes, and I wish I had some *real* bacon."

"Girl, please!" Marvin laughed. He stacked three fluffy pancakes and three strips of fake bacon onto my plate and apologized for not having any real bacon. Then he scolded me for being a pig eater.

I complimented Marvin's wife's good cooking. Marvin complimented my good looks. He was a charmer. He made intimate eye contact and cracked good jokes and revealed how intelligent he was in an effortless manner. He made me feel like we were on a date. He made me feel interesting. He made me feel gorgeous. He made me forget he was married.

Marvin wrote down my information after we finished eating and said he would send me an invitation in the mail within the next two weeks, regarding a party he was throwing at the restaurant. He begged me to come. I promised him I would. I didn't want to leave. I was still savoring our delicious discussion. But the pancakes were long gone and the conversation was about to get naughty and his wife was waiting on him and my mother was waiting on me. I would have to resort to savoring our delicious memories instead. Besides, Marvin was fronting like he didn't cheat on his wife and I was fronting like I didn't date married men. So I said good-bye and looked forward to attending Marvin's party at the restaurant. I hoped I could wait that long. Luckily, I didn't have to.

Marvin called me the next day. I said *the next* day. Likable, unavailable gods *never* call the next day. I was beside myself with excitement. He wanted me to come up to the restaurant and have lunch with him later on that week. I forgot that he was married and suggested tomorrow. He agreed. I was wrong. And I knew it. But I couldn't help myself. I wanted to go up there at that very moment. But I didn't want to play myself. So I talked on the phone with Marvin for over an hour instead. Then his wife came into the restaurant. I heard her chipper voice through the phone. She asked Marvin if he was ready to go. He told her yes and that he'd be out in a minute. That was her cue to go back outside and get in the car. She did so quietly. All I heard was the door close. I love a woman who knows her place.

"Sorry about that," Marvin whispered into the phone.

"That's all right," I said in an understanding tone.

"I'll see you tomorrow?" he asked.

"You sure will," I responded.

"Twelve o'clock?"

"Twelve o'clock."

"I'm looking forward to seeing you again."

"Same here," I gushed, forgetting that he had a wife waiting outside for him . . . until I heard a car horn blasting through the phone, nearly shattering my eardrum.

"I gotta go," Marvin said. "Tomorrow."

"Tomorrow." I held the phone in my hand for a long time before hanging it up.

Tomorrow came. I wore my best pair of worn, low-riding jeans. They cupped my butt just right (thanks to the rolled-down girdle panties underneath). I wore a soft little pale yellow cashmere sweater. It contoured my breasts just right (thanks to the padded push-up bra underneath). I spent for-ever trying to throw my hair up just right, so that the tousled results would look perfect yet accidental. Then I powdered my face and lengthened my lashes and blushed my cheeks and glossed my lips, artificially inseminating good skin and a healthy glow. My brown leather boots and thin gold hoops and skinny gold watch completed the look. In total, I spent well over two hours getting ready. When I studied the results on the way out the door, I looked like a natural, effortless beauty.

I walked into the restaurant. Everyone was watching me as I held my head high in the air. I was on a mission. I looked straight ahead and waltzed over to the counter where Marvin was standing. The customer he was talking to was not listen-ing to him anymore because he was too busy staring at me. I smiled. He gasped and jumped back. Marvin looked up to see what all the commotion was about. I winked at him. He gasped and jumped back too. Then he threw the customer's change into his hand and ran from behind the counter.

"Hey, what's up?" he asked, coming over and hugging me.

"Nothing much," I replied, hugging him back.

"You look stunning," he said, still hugging me.

"Thank you." I smiled, still hugging him back. I scanned the room as everyone stared at us. Marvin was a *bold* married man. I decided to be an even bolder mistress as I closed my eyes and lost my mind somewhere within his irresistible embrace. I'd start by flushing my morals down the toilet. Then I'd to go against my friends' warnings. Then I would disagree with the theory that I was blocking my blessings. I hadn't been blessed with a good man thus far, so what would I be blocking? I'd put in work to steal Marvin away from his wife. He was too fine for me to be ethical. She'd had him long enough anyway. It was my turn now. I'd be patient and accommodating in the beginning as I weaned him off of his marriage. My schedule would accommodate his limited hours of availability due to his house arrest. My bed would accommodate his excess weight due to the ball and chain dragging from his ankle. My plan was officially in full effect.

Marvin and I sat in a booth located in the far corner of the empty No Smoking section. I ordered fried catfish, collard greens, sweet potatoes, corn bread, and pink lemonade. He laughed and told me that I had a hearty appetite. I laughed back, because at least I didn't *look* like I had a hearty appetite (unlike his pudgy-ass soon-to-be ex-wife).

By the end of lunch, I felt as if Marvin had fallen in love with me. My conversation was fabulous and showcased my unique, dynamic personality. My wickedly funny jokes revealed my humorous, down-to-earth side. Marvin's eyes were fixated on my moist lips as I talked. I wondered if my mouth would melt into his during our first kiss. Marvin smiled every time my clumsy hands and knees accidentally rubbed against his. I wondered if he liked it on top of or underneath the sheets. I considered what it would be like once we got on or in the sheets. I questioned how long it would take us to actually get on or in the sheets.

I thanked Marvin kindly for the delicious lunch when he walked me outside. No one was around. He hugged me again before I got into my car. He held me even longer this time as we fell against the door. Marvin kissed me on my neck and said he'd call me tomorrow. I told him I was looking forward to it.

Marvin called me from the restaurant the next day, as promised. We talked for almost two hours. I asked if he had work to do, and he told me that the advantage of owning his own business was that he could do whatever he wanted, whenever he wanted. I wondered if he wanted me to come up there and make out with him. I wanted to come right out and ask but didn't, considering he was the one with all the baggage. I'd put the ball in his court. If he wanted me, he'd have to make that perfectly clear. I was tired of putting myself out there and getting run over. So I decided to be subtly forward in my desire to get with him, but cautiously distant when it came to the actual initialization.

After making no real progress during our conversation, Marvin told me he had to go. I could have sworn I heard a car horn blowing in the background. It was probably Mrs. Chub, ready to go home and get her rib tips on. I didn't ask him when he planned on calling or seeing me again. He mentioned neither. So I got off the phone feeling nervous and exhausted. It was a close race, but wifey was definitely in the lead. After lunch yesterday, I thought I'd surpassed her. But after this conversation, I couldn't tell whether or not I was even gaining on her. I had to catch up. I had to win the race, or at least end it with a tie. But wifey had been training much longer than I had. She held a strong advantage. I wondered if there were any other runners participating in the race. I got scared. I had to find my second wind.

The next morning I told my mother about Marvin's restaurant. I told her how delicious the food was there. I told her that the whipped sweet potatoes tasted like a heavenly cloud. She asked what the hell that tasted like. I told her to just roll with me. She said okay and asked me to pick something up for her. I told her I would. Oops, I did it again. I'd found yet another reason to go up to the restaurant.

I went to pick up dinner for my mother that afternoon. It was only one o'clock. Marvin was in the kitchen. A server went and got him for me. When he came to the front and saw me standing there, his eyes lit up. I was elated. He still liked me.

"What's up?" he asked, giving me a nice, long hug.

"Hey," I breathed, resting my head against his muscular chest. I closed my eyes and listened as his heartbeat gently bounced in and out of my ear.

"You came up here to see me?" Marvin asked, finally pulling away. Then he planted a soft, intimate kiss on my forehead.

"I sure did," I gushed. He had just kissed me. I became a groupie and decided that I would never wash my forehead again.

"You want anything?" he asked.

"No, I'm just picking up something for my mother."

"So *that's* why you're here!" he exclaimed. "You're just using me!"

"Nothing of the sort," I laughed. "You know it's all about you."

"Sure, sure. What are you getting?"

"My favorite. Fried catfish, sweet potatoes, collard greens, and corn bread."

"Cool," he replied. "Let me put in the order, then we can sit down and have something to drink while you wait. You in a hurry?"

"Nope." I could feel my second wind coming on.

"You sure you don't want anything?"

"No, I'm fine," I said.

"Okay. Be right back."

I wanted to dance a jig. But I couldn't, because I was out in public. So I did a very subtle little two step instead. No one seemed to notice. I was trying to contain my excitement. Marvin had kissed me on my forehead. He had held me for a long time and actually kissed me on my forehead. He liked me. I couldn't believe it. He really liked me. Was that the finish line I saw up ahead?

"Let's go sit down," Marvin said as he strolled past me carrying two glasses of lemonade.

I followed him to our back corner booth in the No Smoking section.

"I'm glad you came to see me." He grinned after we sat down, lightly running his fingers over mine.

I bit down hard on my straw and squeezed my legs together tightly. My panties were dampening. My under-arms were prickling. My breath was shortening. Should I feel guilty that another woman's husband wanted to get with me? I didn't know, and I couldn't worry about it right now. I was too busy wondering when he'd file for divorce. I would have to be strong for both him and me. I would have to be supportive. I would have to deal with his family and friends viewing me as the other woman at first. I would focus on winning them over and earning their respect. I would . . . wait. Thought interrupted by some tall, thin, perfect-looking bitch strolling up to our table.

"Hey!" Marvin called out. "How's my baby doing?"

Baby. Why the fuck was he calling her *baby*? Since she wasn't his wife and she wasn't me, he had no business calling her *baby*. But the pet name became the least of my concerns when Marvin jumped up from the table and embraced her bulimic body. And held her for entirely too long. And kissed her on the forehead. And told her how happy he was that she had come to see him.

"I've gotta go," I said as a thick green sensation began to attack and destroy the core of my very being.

"Okay," Marvin said, his arm still around the Bone. He didn't even look over at me. "Your order should be up at the counter. Tell them it's on me."

I stormed out of the No Smoking section wishing I had a cigarette. Marvin wasn't shit. It was bad enough that I had to compete with his wife. I couldn't compete with some stick bitch too. This wasn't fair. There was no finish line. There was no race. If there was, I damn sure wasn't in the lead. Was I even in the running? I had thought I was. Marvin seemed to like me. But he seemed to like the Rail just as much. I was confused. Or was I? I didn't know. Which meant I was definitely confused. So I needed one more opportunity to find out exactly where I stood.

Marvin called me the next day. It was all the added incentive I needed. He brought up how I'd left the restaurant so abruptly. I played as if I didn't remember and casually mentioned the Pencil. He told me he wished I would have stuck around because he wanted me to meet her. She was his sister-in-law. I felt like a damn fool. Marvin asked if my mother had enjoyed her dinner. I told him she'd loved it. He told me he loved my lips. He invited me to dinner the following night. I told him I'd be there. The race had resumed. Marvin loved my lips. He was allowed to flirt with his sister-in-law because she was off-limits. I decided to forgive him.

The next night I headed to the restaurant at about seven-thirty. I was dressed to kill in a silk magenta minidress. Sleek hair, pale gold makeup, and four-inch magenta stilettos completed the look. I was ready for the world. I wondered if Marvin was ready for me.

I arrived at the restaurant. Walked inside. As always, my presence put everything on pause. I looked around, smiled, and put everyone at ease. Marvin came out of the kitchen. He looked at me. I looked at him. He fell straight to his knees. Some of his boys who were sitting at a nearby table fell out laughing and said hello to me. I was already winning them over.

"Damn, you look good, girl!" Marvin announced in front of everyone. "Let me hurry up and order my dinner before I eat your fine ass up."

"Feel free," I said boldly.

"Don't start none," Marvin laughed.

"But I want some," I pointed out.

Marvin just shook his head, threw his boys an *I got this*

look, and led me to a different quiet corner booth. Dinner tasted especially good that night. Marvin's compliments were cooked to perfection. They deeply satisfied my appetite. His humor quenched my thirst. His smile sweetened my tooth. We talked for over three hours. I didn't want to believe that this man was married. It was a hard fact to swallow. And a hard fact to forget. Especially when one of the servers approached the table and told him that his wife was there.

"Damn!" Marvin said, glancing at his watch and jumping up. "It's almost eleven o'clock. I'll be back."

Marvin rounded the corner and walked to the front of the restaurant. I couldn't see him, nor had I seen his wife come in. My food felt like it wanted to come back up. So did all of the nice things Marvin had fed me throughout dinner. I felt like I had just been in a car accident. One minute I was cruising along, listening to love songs with someone special. The next thing I knew, a big rig appeared out of nowhere and slammed into our moment, head-on. I wasn't wearing my seat belt. I felt injured and out of sorts. Marvin approached the table.

"I'm getting ready to get out of here," he said.

"Oh, okay," I stammered. I guess I'd foolishly thought we were going to make a night of it. We walked to the front of the restaurant together. Marvin's wife was standing at the table where his friends were sitting. They were laughing at something one of Marvin's brothers had done. I couldn't get in on the joke because I didn't know any of Marvin's brothers. I hadn't met any of his relatives. I wondered if I ever would.

Marvin's friends glanced over in my direction but paid me no mind. I thought we'd become fast friends earlier that night. Marvin's sister-in-law walked into the restaurant with a woman even taller and thinner and prettier than she was.

"Hey, you," the taller, thinner, prettier woman said to Marvin. She immediately approached and hugged him. They held each other for entirely too long. Then he stepped back and kissed her softly on the forehead. "You look stunning," he told her.

"Thank you." She smiled appreciatively. I prayed that this woman was his sister. But she wasn't. She was his friend's wife, and his friend was sitting right at the table.

"You all ready to go?" Marvin asked everyone except me.

"Yeah, sweetheart," Marvin's wife responded. Marvin approached her, laced his fingers within hers, and kissed her softly on the lips. He'd never done that to me.

"Look at them!" Marvin's sister-in-law laughed. "You would never know they've been together for fifteen years!"

"You know this is my baby," Marvin's wife said, gazing dreamily into his eyes.

"Yeah, you have always been that boy's mama," one of Marvin's friends laughed.

"And she raised me well!" Marvin insisted, bending down and kissing her several more times.

The whole scene was rotting the food in my system. I could have died right then and there. But I didn't want to embarrass myself. So I turned around and walked out of the restaurant instead. I don't think anyone noticed. Not even Marvin.

He called me the next day. I didn't answer the phone. He left a message asking if I wanted to come to the restaurant that weekend for Sunday brunch. I told the answering machine to kiss my ass.

Marvin called several times a week for the next month before he finally got the picture. I never talked to him again after our last supper. I was too mad. Too mad at myself for chasing unavailability. For participating in an invisible-relationship marathon. For trying to run through an invincible ribbon and wrongfully snatch the prize. Marvin was nothing but a flirtatious track that had led me astray. It had taken me entirely too many miles to figure that out. But I had. I hadn't immediately admitted that my intentions were wrong. But they were. And I knew that I needed to start pursuing men who weren't already taken. So I did.

Bottom Damn Line: Fuck a married man. No matter how good your chances may seem, you never had a chance to begin with.

Dennis the Dumb-Ass Divorcé

Have you ever dated a man who was *finna* get a divorce? One foot in the door and one foot out? Still in love but trying to move on? I have. His name was Dennis, and we shared the most exciting, confusing, frustrating, back-and-forth relationship I've ever experienced.

I met Dennis at a friend's housewarming party. We were sitting around her silver-and-white art deco living room playing Taboo, and he would not take his eyes off me. I was not very impressed by his short, stocky, gerbil-like appearance. I was extremely unimpressed by his marital status, which was quite uncertain at the time. Married but separated, to be exact. From my own personal experience, most interested men who were finna get a divorce never did, which is why I decided that Dennis wasn't finna get no play.

Dennis was the Taboo captain of the opposite team. When it was my turn to step up for the win, he jumped at the opportunity to stand behind me, hold the buzzer, and make sure I didn't shout out any illegal hints. His pelvis kept pressing against my backside, but when I tried to step away, he accused me of cheating and moved in even closer. He wasn't slick. I'd figured out the object of his game a long time ago. So playing him wasn't difficult. After my team won, his teammates kicked and chastised him for losing over a woman. He thought it was cute, but I didn't entertain their taunts. Instead I strolled into the kitchen to pour myself another drink.

"Hey," Dennis said, coming up behind me with a cup of ice in his hand. "What are you drinking?"

"Oh, I've got it," I replied coolly, refilling my wineglass.

"Cool," Dennis said, taking the glass from my hand. "I'll carry this for you."

"Thanks," I said politely before walking back into the living room. I knew what Dennis was trying to do, and it wasn't going to work. Trouble was on his breath. Lust was in his movements. An irrepressible scent of drama was rising from his neck. My senses were telling me to run in the opposite direction. And since the nose knows, I did just that.

But when I sat down on the couch, Dennis handed me my drink and sat down damn near on top of me. His thigh was pressing against mine, and his hand rested comfortably on my knee. I gave my leg a quick jerk. He got the picture and removed his hand slowly, but not before lightly running it along the side of my leg. I ignored the slight chill that shot through my vertebrae and took a gulp of wine.

"So, what's up?" he asked.

"Nothing much," I said.

"You did well during Taboo."

"Thank you."

"What are you doing tomorrow?"

"Laundry."

"Do you think I could call you sometime?"

"Aren't you in a, uh, *situation*?"

"*Yeeeah,*" Dennis responded slowly, putting his arm around

me and leaning in close. "But all that's about to be over with. Things didn't work out."

"I've heard that one before," I said. I hated being rude, but I hated being hurt even more. So I finished off my drink, shrugged his hand off my shoulder, and got up to leave. "I'll see you later."

"Damn, that's *it*?" he laughed.

"That's it." I smiled back, walking over to the hostess to say good-bye.

"Girl, why is Dennis all up in your face?" she asked. "He's been talking about you all night!"

"That's too bad," I said. I hugged her and headed toward the door. "I'm not in the mood for any bullshit, so I'll pass."

"I hear you," my friend said sternly. "That divorce hasn't been finalized yet."

"I'm out," I said, opening the door to leave. "No need to further that discussion."

"Okay, I'll e-mail you tomorrow."

The next day I received a group e-mail at work from my friend, thanking everyone for coming to her housewarming and bringing such nice gifts. Five minutes later, I got an e-mail from Dennis, who must have gotten my address from the message our friend had just sent.

Hey sexy, it read. *Just wanted to tell you it was good meeting you last night. I hope to see more of you. There's a barbecue next weekend. Will you be there?*

I wanted to delete the message, but my fingers were a bit stuck. I suddenly felt a bit flattered. No man had paid a bit of attention to me for a while now. But Dennis had a bit too many issues to deal with. So, what to do? My fingers started typing on their own before my mind could make a decision.

Hi Dennis, I typed. *It was nice meeting you, too. I will be at the barbecue, so I guess I'll see you there. Take care.*

My mind kicked back in and critiqued the message. It was cordial and to the point. Dennis seemed cool, so I didn't have to play him shady. I just had to keep myself in check. I reread the message for errors. I reread the message for inappropriateness. I found neither of the two. I hit the "send" button. My phone rang.

"*Girl*," the hostess of the housewarming party sighed, "If Dennis calls my damn job one more time, I'm going to get fired!"

"He just e-mailed me. What the hell does he want?"

"To get with you!"

"What about wifey?" I asked.

"It ain't over till it's over. And since no papers have been signed, the fat lady ain't sang just yet."

"Well, until that big bitch steps to the mic and hits a note, I can't be bothered," I confirmed.

"You shouldn't be bothered," she agreed.

"Tell him when the divorce is final, *maybe* we can talk."

"I hear you—. *My boss is coming, gotta go,*" my friend whispered quickly before hanging up the phone.

Later on that week I talked to another girlfriend of mine who was going to the barbecue. I told her all about Dennis, and it turned out that she'd grown up with him. She'd heard about his defective marriage. I asked if she knew what had gone wrong. She said that Dennis's wife had clamped on her chastity belt several months before they separated. I asked if he'd been cheating and she said she wasn't sure. The truth was being kept tightly under wraps. Dennis insisted that he'd been faithful throughout the entire marriage. But supposedly his wife had gotten an anonymous phone call one day from a woman claiming she'd been sleeping with Dennis. He'd vehemently denied any wrongdoing, but when he came home to a furnitureless and wifeless house a few days later, he knew who she believed.

So here Dennis was, trying to get with me. I told my friend that I found him to be charming and amusing, but I didn't see much happening there. Nine times out of ten, he and his wife would reconcile. And where would that leave me?

But on the other hand, could he have just gotten caught up and married the wrong person? Was he now trying to find the woman he was meant to be with and live happily ever after? Or was he just an asshole who had done the right woman wrong? I had too many questions. So I decided to do the one thing that made sense. I decided to stay away.

Saturday afternoon, as I was preparing for the barbecue, my doorbell rang. I looked through the peephole and saw a delivery person standing behind a gigantic floral arrangement. I signed for it and carried the heavy load inside. When I tore away the paper, twenty-four creamy pink roses came sprouting out at me. Sweet fragrance filled the room. I grabbed the card, totally baffled by who could have sent them. I'd gotten a few dandelion and cannabis arrangements in the past, but nothing this overwhelmingly beautiful. I ripped the envelope open. They were from Dennis.

So looking forward to seeing you today. XOXO, Dennis.

A smile ensued before I knew it. Baby flutters flowed before I could control them. But I had to stop. I had to put my emotions on lock. I had to fight. Hard, like Laila Ali. I couldn't let this married man get the best of me. I had to remember the past so that I wouldn't slip in the present and fall in the future. I took a deep breath in order to regroup. But the scent of the petals blocked the oxygen that was supposed to go to my brain and bring me to my senses. The aroma made me feel giddy and high. My logic suddenly blurred. My mind suddenly boggled. My feet suddenly floated off the floor. But then, even through my natural high, I promised myself not to make one move until I saw the signed papers.

I wore my tiny denim shorts and a tiny white tank top to the barbecue. As soon as I got there, Dennis jumped in my back pocket, and he stayed there all day. I thanked him for the beautiful flowers. He told me I looked good. I told him that he was still married. He asked if he could take me out to dinner. I asked if he was still married. He told me that wasn't my concern. I told him that indeed it was. The sun set. I said good-bye. I tried to walk out, but Dennis was still in my back pocket. He didn't jump out until we got to my car. He told me he would e-mail me. I told him he was still married. He said he was aware of that, was taking care of that, and didn't want to hear about that from me anymore. I liked the way he checked me.

After the barbecue, Dennis and I embarked on an e-mail friendship. He finally stopped hitting on me and started getting to know me by taking an interest in what I was about rather than what I could be to him. Dennis asked about my career, hobbies, and beliefs rather than my eyes, thighs, and bra size. He let me in on the family secrets and marriage woes that even his closest friends knew nothing about. His abusive father, promiscuous mother, and illegitimate brothers and sisters were oftentimes a topic of conversation, as was his frigid, demanding, boring, soon-to-be ex-wife. I must admit, I was becoming attracted to this sensitive, vulnerable, trusting side of Dennis. I relished the fact that our friendship was therapeutic and comforting for him and intriguing and genuine for me. My feelings for him had definitely developed, but I remained true to my promise that our courtship would not begin until his marriage came to an end. Then one day, after a few months of platonic computer bliss, Dennis called me.

"Hello?" I said skeptically, seeing his name on the caller ID.

"Hey, sweetheart. What are you doing?"

"Laundry," I replied, wondering why Dennis had stepped out of our safe Internet territory and onto dangerous telephone turf.

"Come over for dinner this weekend," Dennis said. Not asked. Said.

"Are you still married?" I asked, staying real with my shit.

"Come over and find out," Dennis laughed. "I know where you stand with that situation, so why would I call and invite you over for dinner if it were an inappropriate request?"

"So you're *not* still married?" I asked, jumping up and dropping the stack of magazines that was sitting in my lap.

"Come over and find out!" Dennis insisted.

"Let me think about it," I said, desperately trying to conceal my excitement. Dennis's divorce *must* have been finalized. He knew I wasn't messing around with my stance on that. Maybe the stats were reversing. Maybe a married man who was interested in me actually *had* gone through with his divorce.

"Are you coming?" Dennis asked softly, snapping me out of my thoughts of good fortune.

"*If* I do," I began cautiously, "you best have the proper documentation prepared for presentation."

"I will have the proper documentation ready for presentation, Sergeant!" Dennis yelled. "And I know you *will* come to dinner," he continued, his voice lowering several octaves. "So let's plan for Saturday at eight o'clock. Cool?"

"Cool," I said before hanging up the phone.

Saturday came. I had to dress carefully. Sexy and desirable if the divorce had actually been finalized, standoffish and unavailable if I had been bamboozled. I scanned my belongings and weighed my options: blazing strapless saffron dress or short-sleeved low-cut black dress? I chose the black one. Open-toed, thinly strapped heels or closed-toe spike heels? I chose the closed-toe. Flowing pinned-up curls or straight with a slight flip? I chose the flip. Sparkling evening makeup or naturally neutral makeup? I went natural. Powerful perfume or subtly scented lotion? I went with the lotion. I looked in the mirror. My goal had been reached. I was sexily standoffish. I left my apartment and prayed that the evening's outcome would be a favorable one.

I arrived at Dennis's apartment at 7:45 P.M. He opened the door. He looked better than I'd remembered. Maybe he'd lost a few pounds. He was dressed in a casual dark gray suit. The mixture of the cologne I smelled when he held me close and the steamy spices floating from the kitchen was delicious. Dennis stepped back and told me I looked beautiful. I held my hand out and asked for the documentation. He laughed, took my hand in his, and led me inside.

His vintage apartment was decorated with antique pieces and dark, eclectic furniture. After a tour and a couple of drinks, Dennis took me into the dining room. Freshly cut yellow tulips in a crystal rectangular vase served as the centerpiece on the table. He pulled my chair out for me. Then he walked into the kitchen. He came out carrying two plates topped with jerk chicken and spicy rice. He sat them down on the table, then walked back into the kitchen. He came out carrying two bottles of Red Stripe beer. I spread my linen napkin over my lap. Dennis did the same. Then he held out both his hands. I held them gently. He bowed his head and said grace. I smiled and followed suit.

Dennis's dinner was delicious. Our conversation was even better. We talked about absolutely everything. We drank absolutely too much. By dessert, we were both falling out of our chairs with laughter. I almost fell face-first into my bowl of banana pudding. Dennis grabbed my hand and led me into the living room. He sat me down on his plush velvet couch. He turned the lights down low and lit several scented candles. A Will Downing CD began to play. My buzz heightened my sexual urge. Dennis left the room. I tried to follow him and see what he was up to, but I couldn't conquer the cushiony couch. So I sank back down, closed my eyes, and tried not to doze off.

Dennis walked back into the living room. When I opened my eyes, papers were sitting on my lap. I picked them up and adjusted my vision. They were Dennis's divorce papers. I turned to the final signature page. Both he and his now official ex-wife had signed on the dotted line. I sat the papers on the table. Dennis grabbed the back of my head and kissed me deeply. I responded in a way that let him know what would come next. He silently led me into the bedroom. I lay down. He removed my clothes and caressed my skin softly. His lips touched me everywhere. He sucked my toes. He turned me over onto my stomach. He propped me up. He maneuvered his tongue from the nape of my neck to the bottom of my spine. Then it went where no man's tongue had ever gone before. I lost count of the number of orgasms I experienced. Dennis turned me over onto my back. He made slow, sweet, passionate love to me. He wanted nothing in return. All he wanted was to please me. Dennis whispered in my ear and told me he loved me. I wanted to say the same but I choked on my tears. He turned me over onto my stomach again. He propped me up again. His organ went where no man's organ had ever gone before. He didn't even ask. He didn't have to. The pain was somehow pleasurable. Somehow excruciatingly wonderful. I came again.

I spent the night with Dennis. Hours of slumber passed and he never let go of me. He made breakfast the next morning. Dennis told me he wanted to be with me over bacon, eggs, bagels, and coffee. But he said that he needed some time. He was still trying to mend from his broken marriage. I told him that I understood. That I'd be there as a friend. And that I loved him, too.

The next eight months were filled with a wondrous love shared between Dennis and me. We did everything together. Ate, slept, drank, read, chilled, everything. But then one day, things started to change. The hints that I'd been dropping to Dennis about us seriously committing to each other were now seriously being ignored. He kept saying that he still wasn't ready. I decided to be a little more understanding and patient. Just as he'd told me, I hadn't been through a divorce, so I didn't know how difficult it was. I accepted that, because I loved Dennis and wanted things to work between the two of us. I knew nothing came easy, so I was willing to strive to keep things together.

But then things started to get worse. I'd call Dennis's house when he was supposed to be home and he wouldn't answer the phone. At first I thought nothing of it, but as the problem persisted, so did my intuition. I began thinking that he was doing to me what he'd done to others when I was at his place, which was turn off his ringer to block their calls. On the days that this would happen, I wouldn't hear back from him until the next morning. Signs of an overnight guest were hanging all up in my face, but I pushed them away and kept on moving.

Suddenly, when the two of us were together and Dennis' pager would go off, he'd leave abruptly, claiming that his sick grandmother needed something to eat or that his drunken aunt needed a ride home. Our dates and our time together were becoming scarce. I thought that as time moved on, Dennis would recover from his failed marriage and rejoice in our relationship, just as he'd promised. But the complete opposite was happening. As time progressed, our relationship digressed. I'd thought that the hard part was over. The divorce had been finalized. His attention should have been undivided. His commitment should have been wholehearted.

Eventually our relationship diminished even further. Dates and times together became damn near nonexistent. Dennis's infrequent phone calls came in no earlier than midnight. And they were always invitations to his place. I'd go, but I no longer felt comfortable and welcome there. I no longer enjoyed spending the night with him after the time his pager went off and he put me out because of a needy relative. I was getting fed up. But I was a trouper. A fighter. Laila Ali. I wanted to hang in there. Make sure I wasn't just seeing things. Make sure the accusations weren't just my imagination, as Dennis had suggested. But one evening, one ill, unfortunate evening, the evidence came tumbling right down in my face.

The International Film Festival had come to town. I'd gotten tickets. I was looking forward to seeing a friend's film. Dennis backed out at the last minute. I verbally understood yet silently cursed him. I called my best friend and extended a last-minute invitation. She accepted.

The festival was wonderful. My friend's love story had me feeling revitalized. I was ready to plan a weekend getaway with Dennis so that we could relax, recoup, and regroup. It was time to stop the relationship, turn it around, and head it in the right direction.

After the movie, I skipped through the parking lot toward my car. I was so busy laughing that I didn't notice the speeding truck that shot from around a corner and almost hit me. I screamed. I looked up. It was Dennis. He was not alone. A fat bitch was sitting in his passenger seat.

Time froze. I froze. Dennis froze. He and I must have stared at each other in shock for at least an hour. Then anger, betrayal, and resentment thawed me out. I could move again. I could scream again. So I did. Then I jumped up onto the hood of Dennis's truck. I banged against his windshield with both hands. I reached around into the driver's window and punched him in the face.

Dennis could move again, too. He hit the accelerator. He jerked the wheel to try to throw me off the car. He was actually trying to kill me and at the same time explain who I was to the petrified fat bitch with the played-out wrapped bob, black lip liner, and staircase chin.

I didn't die. I didn't even fall. Instead I bloodied up Dennis's face with my acrylic nails. My French manicure turned red. Dennis eventually stopped the truck. He got out. The fat bitch stayed in and locked the doors. My best friend ran to get my car. Dennis tried to apologize. I wouldn't accept it. I asked if the fat bitch was his wife. He said no. I slapped the shit out of him. I would have been a bit more understanding if the fat bitch had been his wife. She's the one I'd been wasting my time worrying about. But instead I should have been worrying about this twenty-one-year old, jalopy college dropout who lived with her parents and had no job. Who knows, maybe she gave good head. But that was no excuse. For I did, too.

My best friend pulled up. I kicked Dennis in his stubby shin and got in the car. When we pulled away, the fat bitch got out of the truck and came to Dennis's rescue, a day late and a dollar short. I cried the whole way home. Thank God my friend lived right around the corner from me. She dropped herself off. She kissed me good night and apologized for Dennis's behavior. She told me I should consider lesbianism. I agreed, considering how tired I was of dicks. Ellen DeGeneres suddenly popped into my head. I scooted over into the driver's seat. I drove home. I entered my apartment. I did the unthinkable. I called Dennis. I guess I wasn't as tired of dicks as I'd thought.

Surprisingly, he was already home. Alone. He wouldn't stop apologizing. But he wasn't apologizing for dating someone else. He was apologizing for not telling me about her. I told him I couldn't believe he was dating such a fat bitch when he had me. I told him I hoped he wasn't fucking her up her fat ass. I told him I'd wanted to kick her fat ass when I'd seen her stuffed in that passenger seat. That was *my* seat. And Dennis was *my* man. Regardless of what he thought. I'd been sharing the past year of my life with him. I'd gone through his divorce with him. I'd nurtured him back to life. Dennis interrupted my caregiving thoughts and asked me to come over. I was supposed to say *hell no*. Instead I said I was on my way. That's when I bent over and fucked my own self up the ass.

A nude Dennis answered the door when I arrived at his

apartment. Candlelight had turned his dark apartment deep orange. Wineglasses sat on the table by his bed. I fell onto fresh sheets. The scent of vanilla candle wax filled my nostrils. I inhaled deeply. Grabbed a glass. Took a sip. Tried to forget. But I couldn't. Wanted to pretend. But I was a realist. Wanted things to change. But I was no magician. Wanted to feel happy. But that seemed impossible. Dennis lay down next to me. I wanted him to get up. Dennis took my clothes off. I felt overexposed. Dennis's tongue went where only his tongue had gone before. I didn't budge.

I felt disgusting. Ashamed. Used. I wondered who else had been in this bed. I wondered who else had been caressed there with Dennis's tongue. I cringed. I rolled over so abruptly when Dennis tried to kiss my mouth that I fell on the floor. I knocked down several candles. The curtains caught on fire. Dennis jumped up and started screaming like a siren. I grabbed my dress and shoes and strolled into the living room. He had no fire extinguisher. I offered no assistance. He ran to the kitchen and grabbed a pot of water. I got dressed and waited for him to extinguish the fire. When he had, he came into the living room and asked what the fuck was wrong with me. I could barely see him through the thick, dirty smoke. I coughed in his face and told him good-bye. He told me he was pissed but wanted me to stay. He would change. He could change. He just needed some time to do his thing. I was just asking for too much right now. I didn't have to worry about paying for the burnt curtains. He'd handle it.

The thick smog hadn't clogged my mind. I was officially outraged. I came up with a great idea. I grabbed Dennis's hand and led him back into the bedroom. I laid him down. I climbed on top of him. I kissed his lips and licked his neck. I went down farther. I stopped right above his prize. I teased him with my teeth. He moaned and squirmed and pushed my head down farther. I slapped his hand away and noticed how hard he was. I smiled and told him I'd be right back. He smiled and told me to hurry up. I walked out of the bedroom and closed the door softly behind me.

I tiptoed into the living room. I gently knocked down every goddamn lit candle around the room. I watched to make sure that the fire had started properly. When it had, I tiptoed out of the apartment. On the way to my car, I wished I had put a chair up against Dennis's bedroom door. On the way home, I wished I had put him to sleep, then lit his mattress on fire.

The next day, the hostess of the housewarming party called to tell me that Dennis's apartment had been burned in a fire the night before. I acted totally surprised. She said that his apartment was the only one in the building that had been damaged. I was happy to hear that. She said that Dennis hadn't been injured. I wasn't happy to hear that.

Eventually word got out that I was the one who had set the apartment on fire. I heard that Dennis wanted to come after me. But he was scared. Because he knew I was crazy. He knew I would kill him. So he obtained a restraining order against me instead.

Bottom Damn Line: Fuck a burnt-up, confused divorcé. His misleading antics will have you hot around the collar.

IV

The Big Payback

Though she may herself burn,
she delights in her lover's torment.
—JUVENAL

The Big Payback

Patience. It is indeed a virtue. A gift. A necessity for safe, healthy living. Patience is a mediator that calms the most violent forces. Soothes the most hostile environments. Prevents the most dastardly deeds. Patience is to the world what safety boats were to the *Titanic*. With enough of it, you can spare many lives. Without enough of it, there is bound to be disaster. Which is what the final section of this book is about. Bad situations that, depending on the amount of patience administered, could lead to disaster.

Many life experiences require patience. First encounters, for example. Whether they are good or bad, they require patience. If a first encounter is good, then we must wait patiently to find out whether or not it will lead to something spectacular. We must calm our hope. Soothe our nervousness. Prevent premature expectations. If a first encounter is bad, then we must patiently pray that we keep our dignity and composure. We must calm our anger. Soothe our frustration. Prevent a catastrophe.

Relationships. Relationships require patience. When we are involved in relationships, we form partnerships. When we form partnerships, there is no longer such as thing as *me*. There is no longer such a thing as *you*. There is only such a thing as *us*. Along with *us* comes benevolence. *Us* means sharing. *Us* requires accepting. *Us* equals compromising. *Us* demands forgiving. But sometimes we don't feel like sharing. Sometimes we'd rather reject than accept. Sometimes we feel too selfish to compromise. Sometimes we'd rather leave than forgive. But we're in a relationship. We've committed to *us*. So we must exercise patience.

Love. Another entity that requires patience. When we love someone, our emotions intensify. When our emotions intensify, we sometimes become obsessive. When we become obsessive, we tend to want to become the people who we love. When we become the people who we love, we tend to ignore all of the things that we dislike about them. But the things that we dislike about them are unavoidable, because they are now a part of who we are. We must now accept that person's issues, characteristics, attitudes, and mannerisms. We must now accept the good with the bad. We are now faced with new joys to behold as well as new demons to fight. New stories to tell as well as new lies to detect. New sex to have as well as new orgasms to fake. Love puts demands on our level of tolerance. It forces us to calm our impulses. Soothe our neuroses. Prevent our insecurities.

But what do we do when our wells of patience run dry? When we've been through predicament after predicament and have finally had it up to here? When we want to prove to the world that we're tired of being fucked up the ass without lubricated permission? We lose our goddamn minds, that's what we do.

We stand in the middle of a crowded party, bold as shit and fine as hell, *daring* somebody to walk up and fuck with us. If they do, a detrimental injury may ensue, one that will induce excruciating paralysis. It will be the first and last encounter the rueful victim will ever experience with us. Guaranteed.

Say we fall in hate with someone we loved just a minute ago. Say added anger develops because we suddenly realize that we didn't patiently consider whether or not the motherfucker was even worth our time to begin with. Say our last bit of patience was withdrawn sometime last week during a heated argument. So today we have no more. Today we're involved in an even hotter argument. We may perform an act so gruesomely disgusting that it could curdle even the freshest courtship.

Would happen. *Could* happen. Try *did* happen. I experienced all of these things. I got fucked with, fucked over, and treated like shit. On three major occasions. Which was when I lost all forms of patience. All ideas of calm. All thoughts of soothing. All hopes of prevention. I got mad. I needed redemption. So I got even. Extremely even. Violently even. Fuck *even*; I won. First place. Turn the page. Find out how.

Horace the Human Ape

Have you ever met a human ape? I have. His name was Horace, and he was the ugliest motherfucker I had ever seen. Believe that. And I'm not talking about an unattractive or unpleasant type of ugly. I'm talking about that butt-ass, ferocious, a-face-a-mama-couldn't-even-love type of ugly. Heinous. Hideous. Atrocious. Horrendous. I could go on, but I'd never finish this chapter.

Now, we all know that everyone didn't get his or her fair share of physical beauty when the looks were being handed out in the Upper Room. Some of us took what rightfully belonged to others. This is how that "one to ten" scale came into existence. And by the way, you nines and tens need to give those ones and twos they shit back! But anyway, we all know that's not going to happen. Which is why society came up with that *Beauty Comes from Within* slogan. Its purpose is to provide the physically inept with another way to redeem themselves. So when you meet beastly-looking people with magnificent personalities, you forget all about their monstrous appearances and focus on *What Comes from Within*. Unfortunately, that shit didn't work for Horace the Human Ape. His innards were just as vile, repulsive, revolting, and offensive as his outtards, which is why I don't feel the least bit bad about running his ass down.

Horace was an asshole. There's no other way to describe

him. He was a pure, unadulterated, first-rate asshole. The man came from a good, loving family, pledged a strong, close-knit fraternity, and *supposedly* pulled his fair share of good-looking women. Yet he still felt the need to act a complete fool. Why, you ask? Because he was so goddamn ugly, that's why.

Horace was *fully* aware of how ugly he was too. Therefore, he used Mafia-type tactics in order to get attention and ass. When he met women, he'd immediately start talking crazy and acting vulgar in order to throw them off and make them forget how unsightly he was. Horace hid his insecurities behind a fraudulent shield of rude, arrogant confidence. This gorilla managed to scare the shit out of every woman he met via the visual attack that his physical makeup initially inflicted upon them, followed by the abusive rhetoric that hurled from his massive tongue. Horace was immense, overbearing, and didn't mind pressing his big, fleshy body up against yours and asking you things like "Who the fuck do you think you are?" or "Why the fuck are you talking to me?" or even "What the fuck are you *wearing* with your fat ass?"

I met Horace one night at an after-work cocktail party. When I saw his flabby ass bouncing toward me, I knew someone had just unlocked the gates of hell. Horace's head resembled that of the half-moon man's in the old McDonald's commercial. You know the one: "When the clock strikes . . ." His head was extremely sharp and pointy at the top, then spread out good and wide in the middle, and sharpened back up to a point at the bottom.

Horace's eyes bulged out like Doug the Heinous Dragon's

belly. And the mouth. Imagine two folds of pasty, chapped flesh, one stacked on top of the other, divided by a set of bulky teeth that jutted out and curved around like an over-sized boomerang. His long, pointy, dense tongue got in the way of his words and caused a stutter-filled speech impedi-ment. To sum things up, the complete oral package reminded me of Bubba's in *Forrest Gump*. Except Horace's grill was much more severe.

His sorrel complexion looked unhealthy, haggard, and wan. His short, neglected, dusty hair resembled the bottom of a barbecue pit the day after the Fourth of July, when all that's left are burnt, dusty charcoal droppings. And it stood straight up like the needles on a defensive porcupine's ass.

And the *body*. Horace's shoulders slumped so low that his crusty elbows scratched up against the sides of his knees, and his scabby knuckles scraped the ground that he walked on. Through his shirt, Horace's blubbery man-breasts appeared to be about a size 44D. By not wearing a bra, the chimp encouraged his droopy tits to swing about freely, so that his nipples could tickle and stimulate his groin area. His gut, which could surely be found by lifting one or both of his bobbling boobs, was made up of mounds and mounds of flesh. Rolls on the sides, rolls in the back—just a greedy can-nibal's dream.

Now for the ass. Horace's ass was about four inches tall and four *feet* wide. It was such a sick, thick, *wide* sight to behold. This ass was the type of thing that when you saw it, you didn't know whether to crack up or throw up. Now, imagine seeing an ass like that in a pair of tight, ill-fitting, cream linen pants. Imagine that foolish Horace tucked his shirt inside the pants instead of letting it hang loose to cover up that atrocious backside. Imagine that the linen pants were being fiercely penetrated by *each* and *every* crease and crack surrounding the ass, meaning the crease underneath the left cheek, the crease underneath the right cheek, and the crack right down the middle. I'm telling you, the pants were lodged so tightly within the creases and crack of Horace's ass that I thought the boy might catch on fire from all the heat, tension, and friction being generated.

When the big goon came all up in my personal space, I cringed and backed my ass up like a punk bitch in the penitentiary.

"What's up," he said forcefully, his lower lip flailing around haphazardly. "What chu on?"

"*Excuse* me?" I asked, surprised by his approach and annoyed by his demeanor.

"What's *up*? What chu *on*?" he repeated, much louder. "*Damn*, did I st-st-stutter?"

"As a matter of fact, you did," I said flippantly, crossing my arms and backing up a taste.

"W-w-well, I d-d-didn't on the first two qu-qu-questions, now d-d-did I?" he insisted.

Why the hell was this audacious thing talking to me? What had I done to deserve this? I had just been standing there, minding my own damn business and causing no trouble whatsoever. *Why me, Lord, why me?* There were other women all around us. How come my odds of winning the lottery were never this good?

"Do you hear me talking to you?" the human ape asked, even louder this time, now inches away from my face.

"First of all, back your big ass up off me," I snapped, pushing the beast away. "Secondly, take some of that bass out of your voice when—"

"You got on too much makeup," the monkey interrupted, an enormously toothy grin flashing across his half-moon face.

"Well, my *man* ain't complaining," I replied swiftly, knowing good and damn well I ain't have no man. It was just the right thing to say at the time.

"Fuck that goofy motherfucker!" Horace yelled. "This ain't about his punk ass!"

I stepped back. I was in complete awe of this creature. Was I really participating in a conversation with him/it? What the hell was wrong with me? As I spun around on my four-inch heels and started to walk off, something totally unbelievable happened. The animal grabbed hold of my arm, spun me back around, and held me so close to him that I could smell his hot, leafy, gorilla breath.

"Let me tell you something," he spewed, his eyes bucking out even farther. "I make over a hundred thousand dollars a year, I got a portfolio that puts these Wall Street boys to shame, I got women everywhere sweatin' the shit out of me, I'm above average in the looks department, I dress cold as hell, I drive a foreign luxury vehicle, *and* I own my own crib. I'm an independent man, baby. Men like me don't come a dime a dozen, so you better quit frontin' and get it while the gettin's good. Shit, you ain't all that no damn way," he chuckled cockily, stepping back and eyeing me from head to toe. "You should be happy I'm even *steppin'* to you."

Without saying another word, I violently ripped my arm from Horace's venomous grip. I'd been patient long enough. I'd had it up to here. I pulled my stun gun out of my Prada bag. I turned it on and began shocking the shit out of Horace. He suddenly became a trembling paraplegic. His saucer eyes rolled toward the back of his half-moon head. His big ass fell to the floor and began squirming around mercilessly. His cream linen pants were about to bust. He wanted to holler but could emit no sound because his vocal cords were paralyzed. His twisted mouth became wet with drool. He looked as if he were having an orgasm. Too bad he wasn't. His boys ran over and picked him up off the floor. They glared at me.

"*Do* sumthin!" I yelled, waving my stun gun in their faces.

They did nothing. Instead the mortified rescue team backed away from my crazy ass and carried Horace off to the bathroom. I shook the whole incident off and walked over to the other side of the club to make myself available.

A little later that evening, I was sitting at the bar engaged in an intense debate with a Republican man. Right in the middle of my rebuttal, a hand came down hard on my shoulder and spun me around in my stool. I was suddenly staring death in the face again. It was Horace the Human Ape again. I was hoping he'd been rushed off in an ambulance to the nearest hospital or something. Obviously he had gotten over the injury.

Horace grabbed the back of my chair with his leggy arms

and held me captive. He leaned in close and breathed that steamy, leafy gorilla breath all up in my face. The odor intensified when he began stuttering through his initial statement.

"Wh-wh-wh—*wwwww* . . ."

As he stammered on, I kept my composure and reached into my purse.

"What the *fuck* are you—" he began hollering irately.

Unfortunately, Horace never got the opportunity finish his question. The pepper spray that ejaculated from the bottle in my hand and squirted dead inside his mouth prohibited any further discussion. The lethal chemicals quickly soaked into his taste buds. His bulging eyes froze wide open in shock and excruciating pain. His leathery fingers encircled his scorching mouth with a deathly grip. He was trying to tear off the burn. It wasn't working. He bounced around frantically, his shrill screeching resembling that of an impotent feline in heat. I could hear him over the blaring music. The rescue team ran over once again and shoved ice cubes down his throat. Then they escorted the afflicted victim out of the club without once making eye contact with me. They knew what was up.

"I thought he'd learned his lesson!" I yelled behind them, holding my arms out in sympathy. Then I stuck the bottle of pepper spray back inside my purse and turned around to finish my conversation with the Republican man. He was gone.

I stormed over to one of my girls and filled her in on my out-of-body experience. After laughing and gagging uncontrollably for about thirty minutes, she grabbed one of

Horace's fraternity brothers who she used to date. I repeated the story to him. Lucky for us, he and Horace had just fallen out; Horace had tried to stick his elephantine tongue down the man's fiancée's throat earlier that night. So he was more than happy to inform us of who Horace *really* was.

It turned out that the ape still lived at home with his parents, grossed somewhere in the mid-twenties, drove a dented-up, hot-pink hooptie handed down by his mother, and couldn't claim a single woman on this earth as his. This thirty-something "independent man" was nothing but an insignificant, disgusting basement scrub. The gist?

Bottom Damn Line: Fuck a lying-ass, inadequate subhuman who tries to build himself up on your demise.

Igor the Ignoramus

Have you ever dated an imbecile? A simple, dim-witted moron? A dunce? A ninny? I have. His name was Igor, and he was the dumbest, most shiftless boob I'd ever met. Not to mention he had a fucked-up name.

Igor and I met at a gas station. The minute he opened his mouth I knew we were total opposites. His inarticulate speech and slow diction gave it away. But his cute, sweet, rugged mannerisms captured my attention. I loved his big, gentle, fawnlike eyes. I adored his luminous Morris Chestnut–like smile. His tall, agile frame resembled that of a basketball player's. His midnight-blue Rocawear jogging suit matched his cap and sneakers perfectly. He loved hip-hop. He showed me his extensive CD collection. I heard the bass booming from his woofers. I saw his hips gyrate smoothly to the beat. I was all his.

Igor called me later the same day. I told him I liked how he didn't beat around the bush and play that several-day-wait game. He told me he didn't play games. He thought I was "on another level," and he was looking forward to our "thang" (whatever the hell that meant).

During the first hour of our conversation, Igor asked me a million questions about myself. Nice: a man who was more interested in discussing me than himself. Igor wanted to know what I liked to do, where I liked to go, how many brothers and sisters I had, what my sign was, what high school I'd attended, what kind of car I drove, etc. On top of his basic questions, I went on to discuss my dreams, goals, career path, and how I was looking to grow, learn, and gain an understanding of life with someone significant.

Then, after realizing that I'd been hogging the whole conversation, I began questioning Igor. First I asked what he liked to do.

"Uhh, I like to go to, uhh, museums, plays, movies, and, uhh, vacations," he answered slowly.

I stopped for a moment. Those were the exact same things I'd said I like to do. Wow. We had an awful lot in common. Next, I asked what he was looking for in a mate.

"Uhh, somebody I can grow wit. Somebody I can learn wit. And, uhh, somebody I can understand wit."

I paused. The exact same things that I had said, *again*. I ignored my better judgment. I ignored the dialect and the *uhh*'s and the copycat answers. After all, Igor seemed very nice and attentive. He was just in need of a little guidance.

"So, what do you do for a living?" I asked obliviously.

"Uhh, I work at a car wash."

"Oh. Do you own it?" I asked.

"Uhh, no."

"Do you manage it?" I asked.

"Uhh, no."

"*Sooo*, what do you do there then?" I asked patiently.

"Uhh, I dry off the cars wit a rag after they come out the machine that dries the cars."

"Oh," I replied. It was the only answer I could think of.

Now was the time to end the conversation. So why didn't I? Was I willing to force myself down yet another dead-end street? I guess I was, because I surely didn't hang up the phone. I was still on the whole something-to-do thing. Instead of being honest with myself, defying loneliness, and moving on to something that was more for me, I adjusted my blinders and focused on Igor's cute, sweet, rugged mannerisms.

The first step toward recovery is admitting the problem. My problem: I was being just as dumb as Igor.

After occupation, we discussed relationships. I told Igor I was single. He told me he was single. I told him I was childless. He was silence of the lambs. I blew into the phone and did a mic check, a *one two*. The phone was still working. I asked Igor if he was still there. He said yes. I asked if he had a child. He stuttered, then said yes. I slumped my shoulders in utter defeat. I couldn't win for losing.

I asked Igor how old his child was. He said ten months. My shoulders slumped down so low that they rested on my knees. I asked who the baby's mama was. He said his ex-girlfriend. I asked when they had broken up. He said "a for real long time ago." I asked why their baby was so young if they'd broken up, "A for real long time ago." He said that she'd gotten pregnant *after* he broke up with her. I asked how long they had dated. He said four years. I asked if she'd trapped him by getting pregnant *after* the breakup in order to get him back. He said he'd "Lookeded at it through that types of similar points from views." I just shook my head and decided to discontinue the conversation.

Igor called me every day the following week. Despite the constant tugging at my better judgment, I went to the movies with him that weekend. And we actually had fun. I hadn't been on a date in a long time, and the enormous amount of affection that he showered upon me was much needed. So I decided that I would go out with him again. He took me to the movies the weekend after that. We had fun. He was pretty affectionate that evening, too. We ended up going to the movies the weekend after that. It was straight. He wasn't that affectionate this time around. We went to the movies the weekend after that. It was okay. Pretty uneventful. We went to the movies the weekend after that. I was tired of going to the fucking movies.

This dumb situation just kept getting dumber. Igor and I never went to museums. We never went to plays. The only traveling he'd ever done was when he'd gone to Wisconsin Dells for his eighth grade class trip, so I knew the so-called vacationing he claimed to enjoy was just a ploy to tickle my fancy. We weren't growing. We weren't learning. We weren't gaining an understanding of life. We were stagnant and going nowhere fast.

One night, after leaving the movies, Igor and I went back to his house (I mean his mama's house). Igor's mother had picked his baby up for the weekend. When I walked into the kitchen, a baby bag, rattle, and box of baby wipes was sitting on the counter. I opened the refrigerator and saw baby bottles and formula everywhere. I heard crying coming from the back of the house. Acid bubbled up in my stomach. I had to pop a few Tums and sit on the toilet because of the nausea attack. I had never dated a man with a child before, and I realized right then and there that I wasn't ready to start.

Igor's mother brought the baby into the family room with us later on. The baby was irritated as hell and whining her ass off. I wasn't in the mood. Igor's mother handed the baby to him. His daughter started wailing. It was obvious that she didn't like her father. He looked like a negligent fool the way he awkwardly held her in one arm and shook her way too fast. It didn't help that his eyes were fixed on the television the whole time. The baby's bald head was bouncing around frantically and half her body was jiggling in midair. Despite my own issues, I felt sorry for the poor child and held my arms out to take her. When she saw my gesture, the baby froze, stopped crying for a moment, then kicked her leg out at me and started yelling at an even more alarming rate. I glared at her teary-eyed, red-faced ass, totally offended and ready for her to go back in the other room with Granny. I wanted to cry, too. She was so evil. So was I. But I was the adult. I knew I needed to quit. But I couldn't.

Then the baby's mother called. She harassed Igor and asked him when he planned on bringing the baby back home. She needed him to take her to the grocery store. She needed help hanging up the Christmas lights. She needed him to help her look for a new car. I got so disturbingly uncomfortable from the conversation that I started pulling fibers out of the carpet and scratching my nails down his wooden coffee table. I was leaving permanent marks. I didn't care. Then I heard Igor telling her that he couldn't go out to dinner with her. My whole body stiffened up, and I tightened my toes into rigid, frustrated curls. He started talking to her in secret codes. I slid his checkbook into my purse. I would kindly pay myself out of his account for putting me through this bullshit.

I couldn't understand why I was sticking around. It was like dating a fake-ass, broke-ass, remedial, one-dimensional version of Roger Ebert, minus the analysis. All we did was go to the movies and lie up in his mama's house. All I did was sit up and worry about his baby's mama. Igor was happy. I wasn't. So I attempted to do the impossible. I tried to change him. I tried to teach Igor to stretch his limits and boundaries. I tried to teach him to want more out of life and our relationship. But it didn't work. For many reasons. While I reached for the stars, Igor reached for a 40-ounce. I had graduated from college years ago. Igor still hadn't decided whether or not he felt like going. I wanted to live life like an all-star. Igor wanted to live life like a rookie. I was baggage-free. Igor was drowning in baby mama drama. I had a vast vocabulary. Igor constantly misused semibig words that he'd heard on television. I was looking to purchase a home. Igor was content living in his mama's house. I was looking to advance in my career. Igor had become satisfied with working at the car wash for the sixth year in a row. I had good credit and had always known what it meant to save. Igor had filed for bankruptcy and only knew what it meant to spend. Bottom line: Igor was lax, janky, idle, and the ever-growing brunt of my frustration.

One thing I will say on Igor's behalf, though, is that he was popular as hell. Igor didn't have a whole lot to say, so people didn't mind having him around. He had mo' friends than a little bit. Homeys on every side of town. He was always being invited to a card party, fight party, bachelor party, or get together. I had an opportunity to attend some of these events with him, and I found Igor's friends to be just as idle and trite as he was.

But his boys loved him. *Loved* him. They loved him because they knew he'd never outdo them. He didn't have the stamina. Igor had once wanted to be a professional basketball player but he had no game. He'd wanted to be a police officer but had failed the exam. He'd wanted to be a businessman but had no résumé. He'd wanted to have kids after marriage but had gotten caught up beforehand. He'd wanted to be a rap star but couldn't pen any rhymes. He'd wanted to be a player and a baller but had no mack and a pocketful of chump change.

But for some stupid ass reason that I'll just blame on Igor's niceness and strong feelings for me, I stuck around. I accepted the fact that Igor had given me the "girlfriend" title yet took no interest in any of my dreams or accomplishments. I ignored the fact that he didn't have any dreams and had never accomplished anything. I ignored the fact that my mother thought he was so wrong and not good enough for me. I ignored my friends, who knew I was bored with him and told me I needed someone with more depth and ambition. They described Igor as being just *there*. No presence, no profoundness, just *there*. Nevertheless, I stuck around. Until one night when he fucked with me, which he should have known was a Bozo no-no.

Igor and his friends had been planning a big party for weeks. He was so excited about it. I was excited, too, just because the event was such a huge deal for him. I even turned down an invitation to attend the private opening of a new hot spot in town in order to attend. Before the party, I asked Igor if his baby's mama would be there. I wanted to be prepared for any uncomfortable situations—i.e., some bull- shit. He said no. I asked if any ex-girlfriends would be there. He said maybe one who was friends with his cousin. But she wasn't really an ex. She was just some girl he'd taken to the movies a couple of times. It sounded as if I had nothing to worry about.

I dressed to the nines. I had to represent. I went to the party decked out in a gray cashmere pashmina, a long gray cashmere skirt, and gray suede ankle boots. I took my girl who hadn't met Igor yet with me; she knew only the good stuff. Everyone else had talked too much shit about Igor to join me.

When my girlfriend and I arrived at the party, we turned a few heads in the living room. Igor gave me a quick hello, barely even looked at me, and walked off. I was salty as hell but didn't sweat it. My girl and I walked into the dining room. It was packed. I was polite and friendly as I walked past the gawking guests. They were probably wondering who the hell I was, since no one had introduced me. I chose to keep them wondering.

My girlfriend and I sat down in the kitchen. Igor came in and introduced me to a couple of his cousins. They just grunted at me and went back to their beers. Igor walked off.

My girl and I just looked at each another, not having to say one word. My annoyance was apparent. Her silence was supportive. Two of Igor's cousin's friends walked up. I remembered meeting them at a movie theater one night when Igor and I were out. They were both prostitutes. Salavia and Octavia. Two of the most intriguing and interesting people in Igor's life I'd met. It's fucked up when two prostitutes are more interesting than your boyfriend and all his friends. Nevertheless, they were. They remembered me, too, so they sat down with my friend and me and started talking to us. It's fucked up when your boyfriend ignores you at a party to the point where you have sit and talk to prostitutes. But it was cool. The conversation was more interesting than any I'd *ever* shared with Igor.

Salavia was the thin, mocha-colored, five-foot-four one with a huge gap between her two protruding front teeth. She was wearing a low-cut black tank top that was heavily sprinkled with gold glitter. The top laced all the way from her chest down to her stomach. It looked like a loosely laced sneaker, minus the tongue. Nothing but string and skin underneath. Her feeble breasts were severely underdeveloped. Her long black velvet skirt gripped her legs ferociously. Her open-toed scuffed-up platform shoes were sky-high.

Octavia was the chubby, baby-faced, five-foot-two one. She was wearing a bright burgundy velvet halter top and a matching spandex skirt. Her breasts, back, and gut runneth over. So did the five-inch heels on her stark white pumps that were covered in mud. FYI: it was the middle of winter.

During our conversation, Salavia discussed her status as a beauty-school dropout. Judging from the scent of her tart-ass breath, I figured that blow jobs were her specialty. Octavia discussed her six children. (She was twenty-one-years old.) They both discussed the pimp/boyfriend they shared. My friend and I kicked each other underneath the table. Salavia and Octavia kept looking around as if they were afraid of being arrested.

Suddenly, in the middle of my sentence, the two hookers got up and walked off. My girl and I looked at each other in total confusion. I moved on to dogging out Igor, who'd been in the living room playing cards and drinking beer all night. I should have gotten up and left right then and there. I should not have been that stressed at a party. I was supposed to be having fun. The whole situation was just too stupid for words.

During the middle of my dogfest, Salavia and Octavia strolled back into the room. But something was different. The hookers had changed clothes—or should I say stripped down. Salavia had taken off her long skirt, and that glittery black tank top had become a dress that ended right—and I mean *right*—below her butt cheeks. Octavia had taken off her skirt to reveal a one-piece hot-pants getup that ended in the middle—and I mean *in the middle*—of her butt cheeks.

As they eased through the room, everyone, both men and women, stared in shock. Women frowned and cursed their boyfriends for staring. Men ignored their girlfriends and continued to stare in surprised delight. My girl and I almost cracked up. Salavia and Octavia walked up to a couple of lonely, goofy, gullible-looking guys who were standing in the corner. The men, totally unaware of the girls' profession, grinned and shuffled around in excitement. The next thing I knew, Salavia and Octavia grabbed the men's hands and led them outside. My girl and I couldn't contain our laughter. I jumped up and ran to the front of the house, bursting to tell Igor's drunk, card-playing ass what had just happened. I couldn't wait to see the look on his face when he found out that prostitutes were soliciting customers at his party.

But when I got to the living room, Igor was no longer at the table. I asked his card partner where he had gone. He just shrugged and stared at the cards spread out in his hand. I rolled my eyes and walked through the dining room and back into the kitchen to look for him. Couldn't find him. Then, suddenly realizing that I was about to pee on myself, I ran over to the bathroom. The line was down the hall. So I went upstairs to look for Igor and use the bathroom up there. Still couldn't find him. I stood in the hallway, full of urine and anger, and waited for the bathroom to free up. Then I would find Igor and curse his ass out.

As I wiggled back and forth and waited, Igor's sugar-booty, pansy, pantywaist, sissy-ass friend who lived in the house came storming upstairs.

"What the fuck are you doing up here?!" he yelled. "Go back downstairs!"

"I *really* have to go to the bathroom," I explained, surprised by his behavior.

"I don't give a shit! You are dirtying up my motherfucking carpet! Take your ass downstairs!"

"But the line is down the hallway," I whined, wiggling faster than ever.

"I don't give a shit if you piss all in your goddamn drawers! This is my house! Now take your dirty-shoe-wearing ass downstairs before you fuck up my carpet!"

I was stunned. My bladder was so full I was shivering. I was pissed off, too. Bad. *Real* bad. It didn't help matters when the punk grabbed my arm and pushed me toward the stairs. I felt a drop of urine hit my panties. My good, expensive panties. Then I felt my temper reach level ten. So I snatched off my right boot and knocked it hard upside this motherfucker's head. When he fell to the floor, I grabbed his arms and dragged him into the bedroom. He struggled to get up, but I pulled my .22-caliber out of my left boot and pointed it dead in his right eye. I told him to get his ass back down on the floor. He did. Then I told him to open his mouth. He asked why. I cocked my gun and pointed it at his balls. He squinted hard and shriveled up like a bitch, begging me not to shoot him. I told him to open up his mouth again. He did. I pulled up my skirt, pulled down my panties, squatted over his face, and peed dead inside this mother-fucker's mouth. And I hadn't been drinking much water lately, either. I *dared* him not to take it all in. When I was done, I wiped myself with his shirt and pulled my good panties back up. He choked and spit a little too much of my urine out. I made him suck it all back up out of the carpet since he was so anxious to keep the shit clean. Then I put my right boot back on, kicked him in the fucking head, and walked out.

I was livid at that point. Bitches weren't letting me go to the bathroom. Hookers were turning tricks. Igor was nowhere to be found. My girl was bored as hell by all these imbeciles. I walked into the kitchen and told her we could leave just as soon as I found Igor's stupid ass.

I went down to the basement. The dark, dank, funky, steamy, packed, weed-laced basement. I could barely see. So I went up to every sweaty jackass down there and stared the shit out of them, looking to see if they were Igor's fool ass. Finally, when I reached the last unsearched corner of the room, I found the punk bitch. His pants were down by his knees. He was holding some girl, who had her legs wrapped around his waist. She was bouncing up and down. Igor opened his eyes, looked at me, and immediately dropped the girl. She screamed from the impact of the cement floor and rolled over. It was his baby's mama.

I couldn't believe it. I just stood there, glaring, with my hands on my hips. He stood there, so dumb and slow that he didn't even think to pull up his pants. Infrared beams of terror shot from my eyes. The baby's mama saw the glare of my gun flash from underneath my skirt. She ran off with a quickness.

I lifted my ankle and placed my hand on my gun for comfort. I asked Igor to explain himself. I asked him what the hell he thought he was doing. I really didn't care at that point. I was just stalling, trying to come up with a suitable punishment.

"Uhh, she dis girl, uhh . . ."

"Uhh, I know, she yo' baby mama!" I yelled. "Why the hell were you screwing her?"

"Uhh, I'on know," the boob answered, throwing his dumb-founded hands in the air.

"Not good enough." I smiled sinisterly as the perfect punishment came to mind.

"Don't be mad," Igor said. "Uhh, I got a lot of my peeps upstairs. Can we talk 'bout dis later?"

I just stood there, staring at his gall. Facing the reality of my stupidity. Wondering what the fuck I was even doing there. Wondering why I hadn't gone to the other party. Wondering why I was bothering with this dumb, cheating nitwit.

"Come on," Igor said as he finally pulled up his pants. He grabbed my arm and led me upstairs. "Don't even trip on ole girl. She ain't nobody. You know you my shit."

I could have kicked his ass right back down those stairs. But I had something even better in mind. "Let's go upstairs for a minute, baby." I smiled seductively, wrapping my arm around his waist.

"Straight up? A quickie?" his dumb ass asked.

"Yeah, a quickie. Come on!"

I led Igor into the bedroom where his sissy-ass boy still lay unconscious.

"What's wrong with him? He must be fucked up!" Igor laughed.

"I don't know. Why don't you see?" I suggested innocently.

"Uhh, okay."

Igor got down on his knees and nudged the pantywaist. He didn't wake up. Igor shook him harder. He still didn't wake up. I got down on my knees and attempted to wake him with a poke of my pinkie finger. Still nothing. I wasn't worried, though. I knew the bitch was alive because his chest was moving up and down.

"Uhh, what should we do?" the boob asked.

"He must be unconscious!" I gasped, gripping my jaws in horror.

"Uhh, so what should we do?"

"Why don't you give him mouth-to-mouth resuscitation?" I suggested. "Save a life! Be a hero!"

"Yeah, that would be straight," Igor said. "But I'on know howda do dat."

"All you do," I began, a huge smile spreading across my face, "is open his mouth real wide, then open *your* mouth real wide. Then you press your mouth down hard onto his, and stick your tongue *reeeeaaaal* far down inside his mouth. Then you roll your tongue around and around so that you can unclog his lungs and get the air back in!"

"I can do that!" the simpleton insisted. "I wanna save my boy's life!"

It was the most effort I'd ever seen him put into anything other than that damn card game he'd been into downstairs.

"I know you can do it, baby. Go ahead," I said encouragingly, nudging Igor's head down toward his friend's.

Igor grabbed his boy's jaw and opened his mouth wide. Then he looked over at me, smiled lovingly, and opened his mouth wide too. He proceeded to give his boy the most passionate, heartfelt, intense tongue kiss I'd ever witnessed. Igor rolled his tongue all around his boy's mouth, making

sure that he thoroughly kissed and licked every single corner. He was obviously extremely anxious to save his friend's
life and bring him back to consciousness. Igor seemed oblivious to the pissy backwash and residue that was transferring
from his boy's mouth to his own.

"Meet me downstairs when you're done, baby. You're
doing an *excellent* job!" I smiled.

Igor was so into the disgustingly sexual medical proce-
dure that he didn't even look up. He just gave me a brief
wave and continued to tongue his friend down. I ran downstairs and saw Salavia and Octavia luring two more vic-
tims/customers in. My girl was still sitting at the kitchen
table, now fast asleep. I woke her up and asked if she wanted
to go to another party. She jumped at the idea. She asked if
I'd found Igor. I told her yes and that we'd gotten into an
argument that had left him totally tongue-tied. She cracked
up, not even aware of the full story. I promised myself that
I'd tell her the truth tomorrow.

We walked outside to the car. Salavia and Octavia were now
across the street, kneeling behind a huge oak tree. The two
guests I'd seen them talking to a second ago were now leaning
back against the tree being blown away. I shook my head, got
in my car, and sped off. I was eager to get to a real party, where
there would be intelligent people who knew when and how to
properly perform mouth-to-mouth resuscitation.

> **Bottom Damn Line: Fuck a want-not who can't dare to dream.**
> **He'll only piss you off.**

Cecil the Circus Midget

Have you ever been in a fucked-up, heart-wrenching, drawn-out, can't-leave, shouldn't-stay type of relationship? I have. It was with Cecil, who strongly resembled Tattoo from *Fantasy Island*.

I met Cecil at a barbecue. The moment I laid eyes on him, I thought he was adorable in an Ewok sort of way. He was short, of course, with the face of a cherub and the body of a young schoolboy. My motherly instincts immediately kicked in and had me infatuated with this little cinnamon lad. I wanted to take him in my lap and nuzzle him against my bosom. I wanted to feed him breast milk right from my nipple and rock him to sleep at night. I wanted to sing lullabies in his fuzzy little ears and turn our relationship into a Freudian reality. If only I had known then what I know now. I should have just stopped with the whole pedophile act and gone on about my business. But I didn't know then what I know now, so instead I walked over to Tom Thumb and asked him his name, asked what he was eating, asked what he did for a living, and so on.

To my utter delight, Cecil seemed as sweet as a seraph. He was kind, smart, articulate, and complimentary. He said he liked my confident attitude and aggressive behavior. He said he was surprised that I had even approached him. He didn't feel that he was "my type." He thought a pretty, sassy woman such as myself would be more interested in the fur-coat-wearing ballers and crack-slinging shot callers. I told him I wasn't like that. I told him I was looking for a nice, ed-ucated, legitimate mate. He told me I'd just found him. We exchanged numbers and he promised to call. I thought he was an angelic dream come true. Little did I know that this so-called tenderoni was nothing but the devil's Mini-Me.

The first couple of months of our relationship were what an unbalanced woman such as myself considered to be good. Cecil and I clicked immediately. We quickly got wrapped up in each other. I fell head over feet and was in love before I knew it. Sure, I called much more than he did and kept his mailbox filled with letters and cards while mine remained empty. Sure, I paid for damn near everything and served as the catalyst that held our relationship together. Sure, I was so caught up in the whirlwind of being in a relationship that I forgot to really get to know Cecil. Sure, I sometimes felt as if I were in the relationship by myself. But that was okay. Everything would fall into place. Relationships required sac-rifice. Cecil was my man. I had me somebody. And he loved me too.

Well, one day I finally got fed up. The pieces of necessity that built good relationships were scattered everywhere. My patience and postage were running low. My phone bill was high as hell. Carpal tunnel syndrome had invaded my wrist from all the letter writing. So I decided to address Cecil's inattentive behavior. When I did, he was shocked. He'd thought I was happy. He'd thought I was satisfied. It was our first real argument. He explained that he'd simply been trying to see what *I* was on before he started pulling tricks out his bag. I believed him. Our bogus-ass relationship lasted for a year. He never once pulled a rabbit out his hat.

After a while, I began to realize that Cecil was a Frontster. A follower. An insecure, faceless, fake-ass wanna-be who would do anything to fit in and be down. He was the type of circus midget who mimicked *everything* the clowns (his boys) did. If the clowns smoked blunts, Cecil smoked blunts. If the clowns boozed until they were half dead, Cecil boozed until he was half dead. If the clowns stepped out on their girlfriends, Cecil stepped out on his girlfriend. Cecil would have committed suicide if the clowns thought it was cool. He was a flat, idiotic, soulless wonder, dying for a spot in the light. And I was a damn fool, so anxious to get to Relationship Road that I forgot to look both ways before crossing the street.

Cecil was horrible in bed too. Absolutely *horrific*. His height wasn't the only short thing about him. Cecil was a shriveled little short-dick man. His performance lacked technique. His movements lacked rhythm. His kisses lacked substance. His oral lacked everything. He'd go limp in seconds. His stamina was nonexistent. One good thrust of my hips and he was *outta* there. But that was okay. I knew that relationships required sacrifice. Cecil was my man. I had me somebody. And he loved me too.

Cecil also had a stalker ex-girlfriend. A skinny, bald-headed, gaunt-faced, idiotic ex-girlfriend who strongly resembled Skeletor. The only two things that set Cecil's ex and Skeletor apart were their genitalia and the few microscopic strands of hair that sprouted out of his ex's head.

Whenever I saw this psychopath out, she would stare me down from the moment I walked in the door until the moment I walked out the door. She didn't even take potty breaks. The bitch just stood there, all night, staring at me enviously and talking about me to her friends.

One night I was at a party talking to a friend of mine. During the conversation, I just happened to look up and see that Skeletor had actually set up shop against the back wall so that she could stare at me in what she thought was inconspicuous comfort. Her lawn chair, umbrella, binoculars, and chips were in full effect, and she was watching my every move. But when she realized that I had peeped her intrusive stakeout, she shut down her operation and ran off in embarrassment.

After a while, she started trying to grow her minimal strands of hair out into a style like mine, wear clothes that she'd seen me in, talk to people who she knew I was friends with, and find out whatever bits of information she could about me. Her friends would give me the evil eye whenever they saw me coming. People kept running back to share all the negative comments she'd made about me. It was insane. But she and Cecil had broken up almost a year ago. They weren't even friends. They didn't even speak. I had her absolutely faded. He used to love her, but he didn't anymore. Cecil was *my* man now. He loved *me* now.

Even still, Skeletor's constant antics began to annoy me more and more each time I saw her. She started acting an even bigger ass and making even snider remarks. As a result of my anger-management courses, I decided to remain nonviolent and just talk to Cecil about Skeletor's asinine behavior. Surprisingly, he didn't believe me. He acted like he didn't see it. He acted like he hadn't heard about it.

Then I found out (through a friend of a friend of a cousin's friend) that Cecil was back in touch with the lunatic. At some point unbeknownst to me, they had become "friends" again. I was stunned. I was hurt. I felt betrayed. I remembered a time when he was totally through with her. I remembered a time when he said he'd never speak to her again. I remembered a time when he hated her for calling him impotent. I guess he'd gotten over it.

Then I figured out *why* he'd gotten over it. Cecil had let Loony back into his life because she made him feel important. She made him feel tall. She made him feel like the man he wasn't. She made him forget about his own insecurities and low self-esteem and focus on hers. When she claimed to be infected with the West Nile virus, she called and asked *him* to come over and play Captain Save a Ho. When she needed to vent about her tumultuous childhood, she asked *him* to lend her a psychiatric ear. When she slept with fifteen miscellaneous men right after their breakup, she begged *him* for forgiveness even though he'd dismissed her as his bottom bitch. In the end, her neediness was the water that the miniature pimp's now fully blossomed ego needed in order to get her back into his stable.

As hurt as I was, I decided to forgive Cecil for re-befriending Skeletor behind my back. Because they were just *friends*, right? I could still trust him, couldn't I? I still had her faded, didn't I? Why would he get back with *that* when he had all of *this*? Plus Cecil was *my* man now, wasn't he? He loved *me* now, didn't he?

That was the fallacy. In reality, Cecil became a big man in his and Skeletor's newfound "friendship" while he worked to shrink my soul. He elevated himself by telling a vacant Skeletor who she was while he despised me for defining my own being. He expanded his ego while convincing an insecure Skeletor that she should be happy with herself while he hated me for frolicking in my own spirit. Cecil grew through telling a confused Skeletor what to be about while he detested my own choices and decisions. He sprouted up while giving Skeletor purpose. He scorned me for leaving that up to God. Bottom line: Cecil intentionally avoided his own ambiguous reflection in the mirror because it was much easier for him to look out the window and criticize others. It made him feel so much larger.

After the first several months of our relationship, Cecil suddenly decided that *nothing* was right about me. His list of complaints was never-ending. And unfortunately, since he knew I loved him, he knew I would listen.

First it was the hair. He told me that I needed to cut my long locks and dye my hair blond. When I did (like the dumb ass that I was), he told me I needed to grow it back out and dye it brown again. Then it was my makeup. He told me I wore too much of it and that he was tired of me messing up his shirts and sheets. Then it was my looks. He told me that I was pretty, but I could be so much prettier. Then it was my wardrobe. He told me that my clothes were ugly, my shoes looked clunky, and I didn't have good taste. He suggested that he pick out my things for me. Then it was my body. I needed to lose weight. My ugly clothes were fitting too tight. I needed to lift weights to form definition in my arms and legs. I needed to do sit-ups to tone my flabby stomach. I needed to do squats to lift my sagging butt. I needed to do whatever I could to slim down my fat face.

The remainder of the list consisted of every damn thing he could possibly think of. The complaints stormed through my ears like a hurricane. I needed to eat differently and learn to like more of his favorite foods. I needed to learn how to cook like his mother. I needed to stop cursing so much. I needed to act like a lady. I needed to act more like his mother. I wasn't good enough for him, according to his mother. I needed to stop being so loud and obnoxious. I needed to change my attitude. I needed a new car because the one I was driving looked like shit. I needed to take my career in another direction because I wasn't making enough money. I needed to move because my neighborhood wasn't good enough. I should have gone to a more prestigious college. And so on.

It was a lot to take in. Hearing all of my "shortcomings" from the lollipop kid was overwhelmingly painful indeed. But somehow, I accepted them. I thought that Cecil was trying to make me into a better person. He was looking out for my best interest. He was my man. And he loved me too.

So I went to work on myself. I began fixing all the wrongs that I had mistakenly thought were right. After a while, I was making notable progress. But Cecil *still* wasn't satisfied. He *still* insisted on criticizing and judging me constantly. He even managed to throw in yet another negative element, which was competitively trying to outdo everything I did.

When we would go shopping and I'd have money to spend, Cecil would get quiet, act funky, and dog out everything I purchased. Then he would show up after his next payday with a ton of new gear.

When other men looked at me, Cecil would insist that I was purposely flaunting myself. After I desperately tried to convince him that I wasn't, he'd convince the both of us that the men were probably admiring his outfit or eyeing his shoes rather than looking at me. Yet when we were out together, he wouldn't mind staring other women down or drumming up conversations with them, just to call attention to himself and make me jealous.

When I got a new car, Cecil didn't speak to me for weeks. He didn't resurface until he was able to pull up in a brand-new vehicle.

When I lost weight, Cecil never commented on it. He just suddenly started hitting the gym again. When I got a new job making a lot more money, he didn't congratulate me. Yet when he got a promotion at work, he wanted me to throw a big party for him.

All that was okay, though. Cecil was, as always, looking out for my best interests. He wanted me to stay grounded and down-to-earth in my accomplishments. He wanted to stay on top of his game for me. He wanted our power-couple relationship to be well balanced. And don't forget, he was my *man*. He *loved* me.

Then one fatal, unfortunate, unforgettable evening, the

heavy red velvet curtains closed on our disastrous relationship. It was a dramatic, traumatic ending with no possibility
of an encore.

Earlier that day, Cecil and I were on the phone discussing
a party we were planning to attend together that evening. As
usual, the conversation escalated into a huge blowout. Right
before he hung up in my face, Cecil told me that I'd better
find another way there. Done. One quick phone call to my
best friend and she was hopping in the shower.

As I rummaged through my closet for something to wear,
I determined that my relationship was falling apart at the
seams. Tonight I would pull out the emergency needle and
thread and mend it back together. I would be beautiful. I
would be charming. I would be desirable. I would pull out all
the stops so that Cecil and everybody else would realize what
a wonderful woman he had in me.

It took me four hours to get ready. I dressed carefully,
desperately striving for absolute perfection. My shimmering,
floor-length, strapless nude-beige dress hung flawlessly. My
coiled, pinned-up hair and translucent, ethereal makeup
looked exquisite. I was beautiful. I was charming. I was desirable. I was ready to show Cecil and everybody else what a
wonderful woman he had in me.

When my girlfriend and I arrived at the party, I immediately saw Cecil standing over by the dance floor, surrounded
by his boys. He saw me too, but quickly turned away as if he
hadn't. *Let the games begin*, I thought to myself as my girlfriend and I circled the room.

Heads turned as my legs peeked through long, silky slits. Women rolled their eyes. Men bulged through their pants. My four hours of preparation had not been in vain. Many of my friends and associates were there, so I had no trouble getting right into the mix. I laughed, joked, and appeared to be enjoying myself. But deep down inside I longed for Cecil to come over and dance with me, buy me a drink, acknowledge me, *something*. But he didn't. So I just kept up with my good-time facade.

Then, when a group of guys I worked with came over to say hello, Cecil's short, hatin' ass suddenly decided to hobble over too. And he was so rude. As I began introducing him to everyone, he grabbed my arm in midsentence and yanked me off to the side.

"What are you *doing*?" he snapped, an extremely crunchy look spread across his goblin face.

"Nothing, sweetie. And how are you?" I smiled cockily as my hands straddled my hips. The smile grew even wider when I noticed the trails of drool spilling from the mouths of gaping men who walked by. Cecil just stood there and glared at me abhorrently through his dark, squinty, gremlin eyes.

"So, do you like my dress?" I continued, pushing every little button on his toddler body.

"Not really," he smirked as his piercing eyeballs sliced through my outfit. "That color doesn't look right on you and the dress makes you look pregnant." Then he picked up a spiral of my hair and rolled it around between his runt fingers. "What the hell did you do to your *hair*?"

The moment I reached for his elf hand, my girlfriend grabbed my arm and said she had someone for me to meet. In reality, she had peeped the whole scene and pulled me away from Cecil before I could beat his ass like Tina did Ike that day in the limousine. I only gave her friend a brief hello because I wanted to get back to my altercation with Cecil. But when I turned around again, he was gone. I scanned the vicinity but didn't see him anywhere. Then I remembered how easy it must be for a munchkin to run and hide in a big, tall crowd. So I decided to forget about it for the time being, knowing the hobbit would show up eventually.

After about two hours, I still hadn't seen Cecil. I wondered if he'd left, but then figured otherwise after I saw that all of his circus buddies were still there. I decided to leave my girl with the guy she was trying to take home that night and search for the missing midget.

I looked high and low (I mean low and low) and couldn't find Cecil anywhere. I must have circled that huge room about six times over. I saw his friends, but I didn't see him. I noticed that some of his boys were looking at me like I was crazy, but I didn't care. I was on a mission. I was still trying to get my Tina Turner on from earlier that night.

Then I finally found him, engrossed in an act so repulsive, so obscene, that it curdled my blood and shut my system down. Cecil the Circus Midget was standing in the middle of the dance floor with his mammoth head nestled within the nonexistent bosom of Skeletor the Stick Figure. His oversized cranium was so deeply submerged that it was about to crumble her brittle chest cavity. Her sickly cheek was perched lovingly on top of his growing bald spot. His stubby arms were clutching her starved back for dear life. She encouraged him to stand on her feet for added height. His pixie face lit up with a look of sheer delight. Her scrawny lips stretched into a wide, thin grin.

Is this for real? I gasped after shock ran up on me and sucked the air right out of my mouth. *No, maybe it's just a prank*, I assured myself, gagging. An April Fools' joke in the middle of September. A Friday the thirteenth hoax on Saturday the nineteenth. Or maybe it was just a scene from a very bad movie. *Yeah, that's what it is*, I thought convincingly. But as I scanned the room for a movie screen, popcorn, candy, and ticket stubs, I realized that this was no movie. This was real life gone wrong.

Thunderous clouds of disbelief began to whirl above my head. Icy raindrops of grief began to pound against my skin. Muddy puddles of mistrust swirled around my drowning feet. I came so undone that I had to drift away to try to put myself back together. I floated over to my girl and told her about the obscenity that I'd just witnessed on the dance floor. She excused herself from her potential overnight guest, grabbed both my arms, jerked my body hard against hers, and pressed her mouth so ferociously against my ear that I thought she was going to rape me.

"*Go get him!*" she roared venomously. Then she pushed her nose up hard against mine and looked me directly in the eye. "Go get his *muthafuckinass!* We don't play that shit! Go get that imp! *NOW!*"

It was all I needed to bring the sun back out. It was all I

needed to dry myself off. It was all I needed to turn my ass around and stomp through that crowd like this was *The Color Purple* and I was Sophia, going to ask Celie why she told Harpo to beat me.

Cecil and Skeletor were waving their hands in the air like they just didn't care when I rolled up on them. The other members of their insane clown posse were whopping and pop-locking all around them. Everybody was laughing and bouncing and getting good and crunk up in the place. But then I just *had* to go and fuck it up for everyone.

Fire began to blaze through my mouth. Steam started shooting through my ears. Skeletor saw me coming first. Her bony jaw dropped. Her hollow cheeks quivered. Her bulging eyes protruded. She ran away quickly. The other jesters stayed. Their clothes began to burn. Their skin began to blister. Their lungs turned black. It was then that they vacated the dance floor.

But poor, *poor* little Cecil never saw me coming. The dumb-ass dwarf just kept on bouncing his thick ass and butterflying his stump legs all over the goddamn place. As he continued to dance to the beat of the rhythm of the night, I swiftly approached him from behind and bestowed a powerful karate chop upon the back of his neck. His undersized fingers clutched the afflicted area in agony. He yelled out in pain. I hiked up my pretty-ass dress. I swung around in a rapid 360-degree motion and commenced to kick his feet right from underneath him. His body violently said hello to the little floor. I grabbed Lucifer's Mini-Me by his shiny black leather belt and jerked him back up on his mini-feet. I gripped the waist of his pants and brutally yanked them in an upward motion so that the seams would tear at his balls and rip through his anus. He shrieked loudly and begged me to release him from my vise grip. I smiled wickedly and licked the tears that were streaming down his flushed cheeks.

By this time, everyone had formed a huge circle around us. Security turned up the lights. The DJ turned down the music. Cecil's biggest fear had come to fruition. He was being disciplined in front of a huge crowd, his mistress, and all of his homeys. He wished he'd never met me.

"Explain yourself," I demanded insidiously.

"*My balls,*" he wheezed feebly.

"Wrong answer," I sighed impatiently.

I yanked those knickers so far up that fat ass that the cuffs banged against his ears. I jerked my knee up against his crotch and watched as he slumped over onto my thigh. I balanced him there and pressed my hands down hard against his back. I added an extreme amount of intensified pressure and shoved my knee even farther into his tiny little testicles. I shook my calf back and forth like Michael Jackson. *Hee hee.*

After growing tired of the bitchy screeching and flailing limbs, I released the wounded midget and watched as he slithered down my shimmering leg and fell onto the floor in complete agony. He moaned and curled up into the fetal position. I stretched and reapplied my MAC Lipgloss. His burnt-up clown troop left the party in utter embarrassment. Skeletor stayed to make sure her therapeutic little lover was okay. She couldn't even look me in the eye. I decided to let her go unscathed. I mentally thanked her for being the scissors that had cut the impotent threads of our relationship.

Security turned the lights back down. The DJ turned Michael Jackson's "Beat It" back up. The guys from my job were doubled over with laughter. My girlfriend strolled up and gave me some dap. We pimped toward the exit, arm in arm. I handed a cutie my phone number on the way out the door.

Bottom Damn Line: Fuck what you heard. Payback's a muthafucka.

OUTTRO

Nobody loves me but my mother,
and she could be jivin', too.
—B. B. KING

I met a guy named Harold at the bookstore yesterday. Harold the Hopeful is what I'll call him, considering that we met less than twenty-four hours ago and I still have hope that this might work. I noticed him as soon as I walked through the door. He was over in the bookstore café, buying a cup of cappuccino and bobbing his head to a tune that the jazz trio was playing. His look was very distinguished and intelligent. He was well groomed, kind of tall, kind of dark, and kind of handsome. Navy blue pin-striped suit, nice shiny shoes, neat wire-rimmed glasses, and a calm, confident demeanor. My eyebrows shot up. My interest peaked. But then it fell. Because I felt overthrown by the whole dating thing.

I decided against a cup of coffee and walked over to the self-help aisle. I rounded the corner and glanced at the authors' last names beginning with the letter *Z*. Harold rounded the opposite corner, where the authors' last names began with the letter *A*. We met somewhere in the middle. I looked at him. He looked at me. I looked away. He looked away. I kept my head straight but glanced back over at him out of the corner of my eye. I saw him pull a book down from the shelf with a left hand that bore no wedding band. The book was entitled *A Relationship Guide for Functioning Psychopaths*. This could be love.

I looked to see if there was another copy of the book on the shelf. There wasn't. He was holding the last one.

"May I see that book when you're done?" I asked politely.

"Sure," he said. Then he glanced over and asked, "Are you doing research or something?"

"No, I actually need it for personal reasons," I answered honestly.

"Really?" he said, stepping back, dropping his head, and looking at me over the top of his glasses. "Why?"

I debated whether or not I should tell the truth. I had nothing to lose. If he was interested, at least he would have been forewarned. So I decided to tell it all.

"Well, I've been involved in some pretty undesirable situations," I began, hanging my head down low. "I've reacted to some of them inappropriately. My behavior has gotten violent. I haven't always used good judgment when choosing a mate. Some people probably think I'm crazy." This was beginning to feel therapeutic. I was ready to talk further. But I couldn't. Because I was interrupted.

"I can't believe this," Harold said, sighing deeply and shaking his head.

I thought he was going to spit on me and walk off. But instead he shocked the shit out of me and said, "That is *exactly* what I've been going through! I'm Harold."

He held out his hand. I almost fainted. But I fought off

the weak feeling so as not to miss this pivotal moment. I smiled, introduced myself, and shook Harold's hand. Then I got nosy. "What exactly is it that you've been going through?"

"I don't know if I should get into all that," Harold said sheepishly, shuffling his feet back and forth. "The last thing I want to do is turn you off."

"Please!" I argued. "After everything I just told you? I'm surprised you didn't call the police on me!"

"Well, you asked for it," Harold said, taking a deep breath and delving right into his story. "One day, I let an old girlfriend borrow my car. That night I saw her in it with another man. So I went to her house at an obscene hour, got the car, and hid it in my garage. She called the next day and told me it had been stolen. I told her that was unfortunate, and she'd have to pay the remaining balance on it. She cried, but she paid it. As soon as I cashed the check, I broke up with her."

"No, you didn't!" I retorted. "Isn't that what your insurance company is for?"

"Yes, it is," he responded proudly. "But she was too stupid to figure that one out. Another time," he continued, not skipping a beat, "when I was still married, I found out that my wife had been stealing from me. So I reported her drug habit to her job and had her fired. Then I filed for divorce. Luckily we didn't have any children together."

"Damn! You sound mighty vengeful," I declared.

"Oh, I *know* you're not talking," Harold replied sarcastically.

"Sounds like we've got something in common," I said.

"Sounds like we do indeed," Harold agreed.

"Are you going to buy that book?" I asked.

"I don't know," Harold said, flipping through the pages. "Should I?"

"Are you a psychopath?" I asked.

"Do I sound like one?"

"Yes!"

"And so do you!"

I cracked up. "Well, regardless of that fact, maybe you don't need to buy the book. And maybe I don't, either. Maybe two psychopaths can cancel each other out."

"Maybe we can." Harold smiled, stepping in a bit closer. "Are you willing to give it a try?"

"Are you?"

"Yes, I am," he responded confidently.

"Well, so am I," I declared, feeling as if the air around me had just been purified. "But we'll need to take things slow," I pointed out. "And you need to leave any excess baggage at the door. And hopefully your ex-wife is totally out of the picture. And are you still driving that same car you hid from your ex-girlfriend?"

"Oh, it's like that?" Harold laughed. "Well, to address your concerns, yes, my ex-wife is totally out of the picture. She got married to her drug dealer sometime last year. And no, I'm not driving the same car that I hid from my ex-girlfriend. Now, as for you," he continued, his expression becoming as stern as a school-teaching nun's, "I hope none of your undesirable ex-boyfriends start coming after me. And I pray that you never violently attack me or any of my possessions. And most importantly, if you choose me, then you'll realize that your judgment isn't nearly as bad as you think."

Harold put the psychotic-relationship book back on the shelf. Then he pulled a business card out of his pocket. "Here," he said, handing it to me. "Call me. I'd love to take you out to dinner tomorrow night. I haven't had a conversation this honest and entertaining for as long as I can remember."

"Same here," I said, taking the card and looking it over. Harold was the senior editor at a well-known men's magazine. Nice. "Tomorrow night sounds good." I smiled, looking back up at him. "I'll call you."

"Promise?"

"Promise."

Harold said good-bye and turned toward the exit.

"You're not getting anything?" I asked.

"Not today," he said. "But we'll see how tomorrow night goes. After that, I'm hoping that I won't need anything."

"Same here," I agreed as we both moved toward the exit. "Until then," I said, sliding past as he held the door open for me.

"Until then," he said, watching me as I walked to my car.

So, there you have it, folks. Harold and I have a date tonight. I'm trying to decide what to wear. I'm trying not to get my hopes up this time. I'm trying to replenish my supply of patience. I'm trying to take this one date at a time. If things work out, I'll be content with having a mate. If things don't work out, I'll be content by my lonesome. Either way it goes, I will be all right. Because I've learned from my mistakes. I refer back to my affirmations when I feel myself slipping. I marvel at them. I've memorized them. I live by them. I'll die by them.

Wish me luck. If Harold is the one, I'll thank you kindly. If Harold sucks seawater, look out for the sequel.

ACKNOWLEDGMENTS

I wish to thank:

Cherise, my editor, for "getting" everything and changing nothing; not even the "pee" part. I appreciate your enthusiasm and dedication to this project.

Carolyn and Ashley, my agents, for zealously shopping this manuscript as opposed to burning it due to the astoundingly profane language. I knew you two had a wild side. . . .

Marisa Forrest, my first entertainment industry critic and partner in crime. Your support and perseverance pushed me farther than you'll ever know. Your day is coming.

Elizabeth Lyon, my literary industry expert, for sharing your amazing insight, wisdom, and advice with the world.